Cal Shemzak leaped for his life.

A ragged burst of fire exploded in the place he'd been, its heat singeing the young man on his left arm. He hit the sand and rolled, turning his roll into a scramble for the cover of a large boulder.

The power beam screamed through the air again, kicking up stinging bits of desert at Cal's ruined shoes. Forty meters away the robot grated slowly toward its quarry, withdrawing one weapon rod for recharging, extending another, aiming.

With a burst of effort, the young man got to his feet and sprinted the last few yards to the boulder at the base of the hill. . . .

Ace Science Fiction Books by David Bischoff

TIN WOODMAN
(with Dennis R. Bailey)

The Star Hounds Series
THE INFINITE BATTLE
GALACTIC WARRIORS
THE MACROCOSMIC CONFLICT (coming in February 1986)

STARHOUNDS

BOOK TWO:
GALACTIC WARRIORS
DAVID BISCHOFF

ACE SCIENCE FICTION BOOKS
NEW YORK

**This is for
Carl, David, and Lou Benzino**

GALACTIC WARRIORS

An Ace Science Fiction Book / published by arrangement with
Kirkwood Research Corp.

PRINTING HISTORY
Ace Science Fiction edition / September 1985

ISBN: 0-441-27256-8

Ace Science Fiction Books are published by
The Berkley Publishing Group,
200 Madison Avenue, New York, New York 10016.
PRINTED IN THE UNITED STATES OF AMERICA

PROLOGUE

Overfriend Zarpfrin was seated in a Quonset hut on the thick fur of some animal. Outside, the winds of Nocturnus howled against this protecting metal hull. Zarpfrin found himself shivering slightly despite the thermal suit he wore. Curious, he thought. I was perfectly warm on my way here.

Perhaps this was what came of dealing with a Jaxdron . . . .

"Now that we have decided the probable fate of your human worlds, Zarpfrin," said the alien leader, "perhaps you would care to indulge me in a small board game of my own devising."

"I wish I had your confidence concerning this matter," said Overfriend Zarpfrin, his mind still overwhelmed by the enormity of the past negotiations.

A robot cart wheeled out. On its several surfaces geometric shapes were blinking out light sequences grouped peculiarly in an array of connected circles.

Zarpfrin sipped at his tea, regarding the game before him. Natives of this world—grim, multi-eyed humanoid beings—stood in the shadowy recesses. Overfriend Zarpfrin's robot bodyguards stood by the door.

Zarpfrin used his examination of the board game as a delaying tactic. He had no intention of playing—it would no doubt take much too long, and might give the alien a better idea of how he thought. The Jaxdron, swathed in a robe, squatted across from Zarpfrin, awaiting his answer. This alien, not at

1

all human in appearance, was a member of the first star-traveling intelligent race encountered by humanity in its push toward the stars—a race that mankind now fought a strange war with.

This alien was Overfriend Zarpfrin's hope.

The fate of the human worlds hung in the balance, but thanks to Zarpfrin's machinations, there was hope . . . as long as everything worked according to plan.

"Well?" The Jaxdron's actual word was a garbled crunch of sound. Speakers hanging from webwork translated the indication of impatience into Standard Galactic so that Zarpfrin could understand.

Zarpfrin held up a hand and looked down again at the board. "I am grateful to you for providing for my entertainment, but each moment I spend here is a risk to my control of the situation within my home worlds."

"As you wish, spoilsport."

Zarpfrin suspected that the alien was pouting. He got to his feet. "I apologize, but our talk has been long and arduous, and as you know, there are many matters for me to prepare for. I trust that our communications will continue in the normal manner?"

"Yes," replied the alien. It turned to the board, lifted a long multi-jointed digit, and touched a light-nub.

With crackles and explosions of smoke, the pieces self-destructed then melted, puddling off the gameboard.

"But be aware, Zarpfrin," said the Jaxdron. "Ours is a game that cannot be so refused."

For the first time during the entire session, Overfriend Zarpfrin of the Federation smiled, albeit grimly.

"Oh, do not worry," he said. "This is a game that I think I am going to enjoy."

Gesturing for his robot bodyguards to follow, Zarpfrin walked out into the windy cold toward his starship. Before he stepped onto the ramp, he gazed up at the winking stars.

Soon, Captain Tars Northern, he thought. Very soon I shall have you, the *Starbow*, your crew . . . and my dream!

Chapter One

She dreamed she flew through space, and the stars hated her. The very stars through which she cruised seemed to taunt her, red giants and white dwarves equally cold in the silent starscape.

O be a Fine Girl and Give us a Kill! You are our demon princess, blippie. Yo are the missionary of gloom, our emissary to life with this message. Though of star-stuff you are made, O life, to star-stuff you will return, and we shall mock your silent grave with our eternal furnaces.

She seemed imprisoned within this grim galaxy—no, not the Milky Way with its serene and graceful spirals like a dancing starfish, but a squat, stunted clustering of trillions of stars like some deep-sea creature, scuttling its phosphorescent way in the darkness. She rode her blip-ship—her new one, the XT Mark Nine—within this maze of baleful jewels, for once tripping over stellar gravity wells rather than skating them; feeling pain from the radiation all about her compact ship, rather than thriving on the energies moving through space like invisible rainbows.

Her connections—the biotech jacks connecting her neural centers and her cyborg circuits with the complex but dumb mechanical beast she flew—seemed to itch, and she could not scratch!

The stars, planets, asteroids, and all their attendant

3

interstellar debris seemed to chuckle with one icy voice at the dilemma of this intruder within their midst.

Her sensors, previously displaying a complete holographic reading upon her environs, suddenly shut off, replaced with a skewed two-dimensional view of this dream-corner of the universe, like an old-time movie screen showing those antique "flicks" which Cal would dredge up from forgotten basement archives. On that screen she could not close her eyes to, came a series of snapshot images, spearing her brain with vivid pain:

—identity melding with a Conglomerate on the planet Walthor . . .

—the instant of panic and unsureness at the *Starbow*'s attack upon the *Ezekiel*, fearing she would never see Cal again . . .

On and on these images paraded, a scrapbook of sensations that had led her here to this dark galaxy, this dark dream. . . .

Look upon your kindred, the stars seemed to say. This is the heritage of life—and the only meaning that those who have spawned you have given you is to serve them by killing and killing. . . .

No! cried Laura. *I serve them no more! I am not their pawn! I have thrown my lot in with another cause.*

But the dark stars simply laughed.

Don't you remember Laura Shemzak? You are our Angel of Death.

No! Laura thought, foreseeing the inevitable image that would come to her. *No, I can't take it . . . not again!*

But follow it did, relentlessly, and a moving image too —slow motion: Cal's young face, smiling before her; then the sudden compulsion, the lifting of her gun, the pulling of the trigger, the expression on Cal's face just before he died—

No! she screamed, flailing at the image. *No!* she yelled at these dark alien stars. Suddenly the wires within the snug cockpit drifted up like weightless snakes. They began coiling about her neck . . . coiling and constricting and strangling.

And the stars seemed to laugh, and they said, This is not yet the worst, Laura Shemzak. You shall later curse us for not killing you now!

• • •

Laura Shemzak awoke, sweating.

Her sheets were kicked and sprawled all about her, and she clutched her pillow desperately. Her hair was matted to her face by the sweat, the silken pajamas issued her by the *Starbow* commissary clinging all over her well-muscled body.

—Cal, her brother, being sucked aboard a Jaxdron ship on Mulliphen even as she was doing the Federation's dirty work . . .

What a dream, she thought. She hadn't had a doozie like that one since the cyborg operations had begun over four years ago. She lay on the mattressed bunk of her compartment aboard the pirate/mercenary ship *Starbow*, feeling again the stark sense of aloneness and despair that had flooded her in that first terrible week of operations funded by the Federation: alone, unloved, comfort behind her and nothing but a dreadful unknown in the future, waiting for her like a cowled creature, face hidden.

Like then, she wanted to vomit, but she did not. Like then, she wished she was dead—but she hung on to survival. When her trials had registered years ago on quivering hospital needles, they had rushed her to another room, and biochemical and biotechnical analyses were taken. She had sweated then, too, almost sweated away her very life it seemed, amidst the worried murmurs of the doctors.

And finally, as she lay in her room, her body seemingly nothing but newly bonded rearrangements of stitches and tissue—impregnated now with all manner of alien machinery and circuitry—they had come to her and said take this, it will make you feel better. Take it sparingly, for you will not need it often, but you will need it regularly to quell this experience when it arises.

They showed Laura Shemzak how to take the drug, and it seemed very simple. They had issued her a supply, along with aspirin, and it had simply seemed a part of being a blip-ship pilot.

She went and poured herself a glass of water, shuddering as the cool stuff slid down her throat, still feeling the despair encircling her in a swaddling of nothingness. Every cell in her body seemed to call out in need.

How odd, she thought with what rationality remained to

her. I only took the drug just before this whole affair began. Generally, it lasted much longer.

She put the water glass down, sat unsteadily in a chair, pulled the right silk pants leg up from shin to knee and waited a moment for her hands to stop shaking. Then she struggled to remember the code. What the hell was wrong with her, anyway? Had all this *Starbow* business devastated her brain so much?

Then it came to her. She tapped her fingernails on the appropriate pressure spots, in the necessary order. A small servomotor hummed faintly, and a section of skin opened up to reveal a small compartment. She pulled out a small plastic bag holding about three grams of blue powder.

Zernin.

It was fortunate that the organic nature of the substance blended with the rest of her, or Dr. Mish would surely have spotted this stuff. And even pi-mercs might not approve of this junk.

But she needed it, she thought. She deserved it. It gave her just the right edge necessary for blip-ship piloting. It made her cells resonate with just the right notes to blend in with the songs of interstellar space. She was no addict, she reminded herself. How could you be an addict if you take only a very tiny bit perhaps once in a standard month? It was a necessary thing for blip-ship pilots, the Federation scientists had discovered. And so, they had given it to her, and it had kept her going, this wonderful substance.

As carefully as she could, she measured out a fraction of the powder then put the rest away, noting to herself that she couldn't risk going through another examination with Dr. Mish while carrying the bag. She would have to hide it somewhere.

The biotechs had designed the dispenser for this drug into her cyborg system; it was usually very simple to take her allotted amount, tap open another cavity in her abdomen, then slip the blue powder into a receptacle which in turn would slowly dispense it into her system at the appropriate times. But this time her unsteadiness made the process difficult. All the frenetic activity of late—the chases, the terrors, the emotional drain—must have stepped up the need for the stuff. And she'd forgotten, what with all the excitement, that she needed a refill.

Finally the cavity was open, the dispenser unsnapped.

Shivering a bit, she lifted the paper, creased in the center, tapped the drug into place, and closed herself up. By the time she had her main supply secreted back in her calf, the drug was already kicking in. She leaned back in the chair, feeling the tension ebb away like an angry tide falling back into a calm sea. Things are not so bad after all, she thought.

She now felt peaceful and serene, yet magnificently alert on that private beach of hers, the zephyrs of the universe sweetly sighing her name, all its smells just for her. She yearned once more for the excitement of sailing the starlanes in her blip-ship, but knew that lying by this inner sea of hers would be enough for now.

And the stars above this tuneful surf inside a spaceship . . . those stars were laughing again.

Only this time, Laura Shemzak laughed with them.

Chapter Two

There were only five of the long cylindrical ships studded with
protuberances—a foreshadow of the vast armadas the aliens
were known to command. They slashed through the Kendrick's Vision second line of defense, diving through the atmosphere and laying waste to the city's capital, Shiva, on the
coast of its largest continent, Raj.

President Freeman Jonst was just finishing his breakfast
when the power beams began their strafing runs. From his
view atop a hill overlooking the harbor, he saw the swords of
light rip through his beloved home. By the time he had reached
his comm-unit to command defensive measures, the ships were
gone, thankfully leaving just a moderate amount of wreckage,
with few lives lost.

The Vision's sensors, however, indicated that during their
brief raid powerful analysis rays had been in use—the destruction was apparently but a ruse to disguise enemy reconnaissance.

Freeman Jonst was not the kind of man one took lightly.
Over two meters tall, with grizzled gray hair which looked like
a well-trimmed scouring pad, Jonst was from Chedrow's
World, 1.4 Standard Earth's gravity; his chosen home was
only .9. And if you spat upon his planet, Kendrick's Vision,
you spat on Freeman Jonst and were lucky to retain your
salivary glands. Under Jonst's leadership, for two decades the
colony he had founded thrived on the reputation for harbor-

ing no galactic riffraff, maintaining only marginal relations with the Federation, and trading with other Free Worlds only for the Vision's vital necessities. He kept his planet's integrity and ecology as clean as possible, for that was his dream, his people's dream.

Far from the center of Federation power, with plenty of well-armed Free Worlds between it and Terra, it enjoyed a peace and tranquillity unusual in the annals of human colonization of the galaxy.

That was, until that fateful morning.

Later that day, when Jonst received his ministers and their reports, which showed just how easily those Jaxdron whip-ships had dealt with second-hand fighters and rudimentary defense screens, the conclusion, as much as Freeman Jonst despised it, was inevitable.

He took his cigar, its end chewed to pieces, from his mouth and made the pronouncement that all of his ministers had expected to hear: "Gentlemen, when we settled this proud gem of a planet far from other Free Worlds, farther still from the Federation, we did so with a dream for a solitude. However, with the menace of a warlike alien civilization so apparently intent on conquering us, we have no choice but to seek help. Military help, for as long as these wretched beings are a threat to our peace."

He turned to a communications officer. "Bill, would you come to my office tonight? I'll have my letter to Federation Central ready for transmission by then."

The eyes of the others were lowered.

"Merely a temporary measure, gentlemen," grumbled Jonst. "But I promise you that I will keep Kendrick's Vision a safe place to raise our children and fulfill our dreams. . . . And, at the end of all this, I promise you a Jaxdron head to hang over every mantelpiece."

"But no one knows what they look like!" objected one of the men.

A slow, humorless grin moved over the great man's thick face. "When they're over the mantelpieces, my friend, they're gonna look dead. No one messes with Freeman Jonst's planet! I'd make a deal with the devil to keep her safe!"

Not a soul at the table dared say it, but they all knew that they were about to do just that.

Chapter Three

Cal Shemzak leaped for his life.

A ragged burst of fire exploded in the place he'd been, its heat singeing the young man on his left arm. He hit the sand and rolled, scraping himself on an occasional rock, turning his roll into a scramble for the cover of a large boulder.

The power beam screamed through the air again, kicking up stinging bits of desert at Cal's ruined shoes. Forty meters away the robot grated slowly toward its quarry, withdrawing one weapon rod for recharging, extending another, aiming.

With a burst of effort, the lithe, brown-haired young man got to his feet and sprinted the last few yards to the boulder at the base of the hill.

Shaded for the moment from the glare of this planet's huge yellow sun, Cal sucked in a gasp of dry air and leaned against the rock.

What the hell was he doing here? The thought rang in his brain, an echo of its initial occurrence a mere hour before, when he had woken up in the middle of an alien desert with only a canteen of water, clutching a ragged map which seemed, at first glance, indecipherable.

How had a simple predoc quantum mechanic landed in a place like this? He'd searched his memory and found it as dry as this toasted piece of hell where he now lay.

Bizarrely colored cactus blossoms were scattered on the parched landscape like tapers of frozen flame. Only an occasional stir of cloud appeared in the azure sky. In the distance were some hills.

He knew his name and he knew his profession. But when he'd awoken in the midday heat, everything else seemed to be fried from his brain.

He was given only a short time to puzzle the matter over, take a few sips of the tepid water from the canteen, and scrutinize the map—alien hieroglyphics bird-tracked across what seemed a representation of this land, including the hills—before the juggernaut rose from behind a grouping of rocks and in a monotone announced its intention.

"I shall kill you, Calspar Shemzak."

A simple enough mission. And the damned four-meter-high robot looked quite capable of doing it too. Funny thing, though. In an era when anthropomorphized mechanicals were at first sight indistinguishable from a human being, and battle machines were simply unornamented mechanisms, this thing was an anomaly.

In fact, Cal Shemzak thought, his memory percolating, this thing resembled a robot from one of those hilarious old movies.

It was gray and black, the color of gun metal. Parts of its thick body shone in the sun while other parts were dull. Glass? Plastics? Hard to say, but it was a big thing with awkward movements, steamshovel treads and—

And on its chest were painted concentric circles of alternating red and white.

A target?

Its target, however, was clearly Cal Shemzak. A rod extracted and started firing energy pulses, barely missing Cal. Then, at a relentless pace, it started toward him.

Cal could outrun the thing in a race, no question. A short race, though. For while Cal had to slow occasionally, or even stop and rest when he felt he was out of the thing's firing range, the robot continued rolling along at a steady ten kilometers an hour.

Squinting up now behind the boulder, Cal examined the climb before him, taking precious seconds to regain his breath. He had struck out immediately for the hills, almost instinctively. But as he huffed along, he snatched anxious glances at the map.

It seemed to indicate something of importance on one of

the hills. Something he was supposed to get to, he thought. Safety, freedom . . .

The target on the robot seemed to indicate that it was a weapon. Which meant that this was some kind of test.

Test.

Immediately, even as he struck out up the slope, the word and associated memories struggled up to his awareness . . .

Jaxdron.

He was a prisoner of the Jaxdron! Now he remembered! Now—

A bolt of energy slammed into a cactus just meters below him. He didn't even bother to turn around and look, knowing that the robot was still behind him, knowing that this grade wouldn't stop it.

From somewhere he tapped inner resources and increased his pace. Just a few minutes . . . Just a few minutes more and he would reach the summit of this hill and know why the map seemed to want him there.

And while he ran, memory struggled piecemeal through the dank fog that was his mind.

Cal Shemzak remembered the Jaxdron raid on the Project on Mulliphen; Dr. Ornix's traitor prosthetic hand; his capture by the weird alien ship. He recalled vaguely his time aboard the Jaxdron starship with not even a glimpse of his captors; the strange paces the aliens put him through, the mazes, the puzzles. And finally, a planet . . . but not this planet . . . .

The echoes and images of experience were swallowed by the roar of the robot's motors as they worked harder to deal with the slope. The air was hot in Cal's lungs, and his leg muscles felt as though they were being torn apart; but a quick glance back showed that he had gained some ground over his pursuer. Sweat stung his eyes as he directed them upward and saw the top of the hill, the plateau flat, seemingly just as bare as the rest of this godforsaken country.

What if there was nothing there? What if he had the wrong hill?

He swallowed back his despair.

No. Impossible. He'd figured out the map; that was part of the test. And it was a test—just one of the many given him by the Jaxdron for their own inscrutable reasons. He'd pass this one just like he'd passed all the others.

He hoped.

As though to increase his doubts, another blast of fire dug a quick hole paces behind him; that goddamned robot wasn't giving up, that was for sure.

Cal Shemzak slogged upward, wondering if all this really wasn't a Federation hell reserved for naughty and rebellious schoolboys.

When he topped the hill, practically wheezing with exhaustion, he instantly saw the rifle.

It lay propped on a rock.

He ran for it, the sounds of the climbing robot growing louder behind him.

Just two meters away he stopped cold in his tracks. There was a glass case around the thing, one angle of it shining in the sun.

If I ever actually meet a Jaxdron, Cal thought, I swear with my bare hands I'll . . .

He did not pause for fantasy, instead checking the case, which proved to be some sort of plastic. It completely enclosed the rifle—which appeared to be a standard-issue Federation .50 mm blaster, energy node showing a full charge—and would not budge.

A rock, thought Cal. Maybe I'm supposed to break it. Maybe— His eyes swept along the ground and instantly he saw the puzzle.

It was a rectangular variation on Rubik's Cube. It was clear that if the puzzle were solved, the glass case would open.

However, there was a definite deadline involved.

Cal did not take the leisure to rail at the perpetrators of this madness; he picked up the puzzle and surveyed it, his sharp mind instantly taking in the arrangement of triangular colors to be unified into blocks. In a moment he analyzed the thousands of possible permutations and combinations, and computed the proper method for solving the puzzle.

Certainly was easier than running, he thought as he solved the problem with a few quick twists of his fingers.

With a whirring noise one of the panels of the plastic case opened. Cal reached in and pulled out the energy rifle.

Not much time to go, he thought as he rubbed the perspiration off his palm. He searched his mind for the memory of how to operate one of these things. He never had, of course. Unlike his sister Laura, he'd never joined the military, though he had read books featuring blasters, and seen movies . . . .

Yes. There was the safety. He thumbed it off. The weapon seemed to throb in response, crystalline strips fading into a bright red.

Even as the ragged top of the robot's head bobbed into view, Cal's finger searched for the trigger. By the time the target on the metal chest was visible, Cal was aiming.

The stream of energy caught the mechanical creature dead on, drilling a hole through its chest. It toppled, crashing out of sight. An explosion rocked the hill, and thick black smoke began to swirl up.

Cal picked himself up from the ground, where he'd been felled by the recoil of the blaster. Cautiously, he peered over the side of the hill.

The stench of burnt insulation from an electrical fire was acrid. The robot was quite out of commission, bits and pieces strewn in a trail down the slope.

Then the skyline rolled open, like a matte painting mistakenly moved in a film. Fog rolled in.

The sun above switched off. The horizons died away into blank gray walls, and lamps glowed eerily, like disembodied spirits.

He sees himself in a mirror, and there is a mirror behind him, his image reflected infinitely as he reaches out to touch and all the others reach out to touch him and—

A voice fragmented Cal Shemzak's total disorientation: "Sir?"

"What?" Cal looked down at his rifle, which had turned into just a cheap plastic model.

Backlit as though by some spotlight, a tall figure carrying something on a tray marched slowly into the wierd twilight room that had once been a desert.

Cal could see that the man wore a topcoat and tails. "I thought, sir," said the man, "that you would like some freshly made iced tea."

Cal sighed and slowly reoriented himself.

Of course: projection, hallucination, and hypnosis. The Jaxdron were increasing the sophistication of his mental workouts.

But why? What were they all for? They knew he was intelligent, and certainly they had the power to brainwash him, dissect him, do whatever the hell they pleased. Then why were they toying with him?

"Thank you, Wilkins," said Cal Shemzak as he took the iced tea and drank. Demi-dream or no, this bizarre business had certainly dehydrated him.

"Lunch will be served soon, sir," said the servant. "I believe you just have time for a shower."

Cal Shemzak acknowledged Wilkins with a nod and set the empty glass back on the tray, wondering what kind of drugs had been in it this time.

Well, Laura, he thought, your brother is getting in deeper and deeper.

He smiled to himself. These creatures were damned weird and damned clever. But dollars to donuts they'd never encountered beings quite like Cal Shemzak or his sister Laura.

And Cal Shemzak promised himself the Jaxdron were going to rue the day they started messing with them.

"Thank you, Wilkins. Nothing like a little exercise in the morning, what?"

Chapter Four

"You've got a black hole for a brain if you think I'm going to get on an operating table for that guy," Laura Shemzak said. Her black hair was longer now and she had a new habit of running her left hand through it.

"Laura, now that Dr. Mish has . . . uhm . . . reassembled and reoccupied his . . . shall we say, mobile unit," countered starship captain Tars Northern impatiently, "there is no reason whatsoever that the implant the Federation placed in you should not be removed."

"Yeah, but which one?" Laura said. "I've got so god-damned many, how is he going to know he won't shut off my speech modulators or something!"

Silver Zenyo looked up from her meal, smiling nastily. "Oh, but that would be a blessing!"

"Shut up, you painted bitch!" Laura said, her dark eyes flashing at the exotically dressed officer. Laura wore her usual black jumpsuit and blood-red scarf.

"Now ladies," said Northern with a mollifying gesture. "Laura, now that you are a member of the crew, you've got to have more respect for your shipmates. And Silver—you can well understand Pilot Shemzak's feelings about biotech operations. Remember her experience on Baleful, shooting her own brother as she was secretly programmed to do by Overfriend Zarpfrin and the Federation."

"It wasn't her brother, it was a copy," Silver said, daintily dabbing her lips with a napkin. "A cyborg copy of Cal Shemzak, just like the other pair of copies we've got hidden away so that our gentle blip-ship pilot doesn't plug them as well!"

Laura opened her mouth to shoot another insult at the midshipman from Morpheus Three, but stopped herself. She looked over to Dr. Michael Mish, the robot body that externalized the consciousness of the artificially intelligent starship she sat in, the *Starbow*. Dr. Mish wore a white silk jacket and floppy bowtie, his mane of white hair and kind eyes making him look like a kindly grandfather in one of those old movies she and her brother Cal used to watch.

Laura reminded herself she had promised to trust these people. Besides, as much as she hated to admit it, Silver was right. She had to get this goddamn device off her optic nerve.

She sighed and nodded. Uncharacteristically mute and sullen, she stared at her mystery meat grown in the hydroponics section, her mind ranging back over what she had been through in the last month.

After finishing an Intelligence mission on Walthor, she had discovered that the mysterious Jaxdron—the only other intelligent species in the galaxy with stardrives and weaponry sophisticated enough to challenge the might of the Federation and the separate autonomies of the Free Worlds—had raided an experimental Federation station on Mulliphen. Mulliphen was close to the Fault, a weakness in the fabric between normal space, underspace, and the complex array of potential different dimensions. They had destroyed the Causal-Field Generator that attempted to explore these strange intersections of time and space, and had kidnapped her brother Cal.

Federation officials had at first been reluctant to grant her permission to acquire a blip-ship—a small, experimental starship she had been surgically altered to pilot—and pursue her captured brother. "Hopeless" was the term Friend Chivon Lasster had used. But hopeless or not, Laura knew she had to try, that she had to fall back upon her unique intuitive abilities to rescue Cal. Then Overfriend Zarpfrin had interceded, dispatching her to the planet Shortchild to be assigned the latest model of the XT blip-ship line. From there she was to proceed to where sensors showed that the Jaxdrons seemed to be headed: Baleful, one of the few human-colonized worlds the aliens had actually captured in the five standard years of the First Galactic War.

However, the freighter *Ezekiel*, conveying her to Short-child, was attacked and put out of action by a group of pimercs—pirate/mercenaries—under the command of this strange man, Captain Tars Northern. Northern was well-known by Overfriend Zarpfrin and Friend Lasster. Years before, his ship *Starbow* had apparently been one of several experimental artificially intelligent starships, a project headed by Zarpfrin. Chivon Lasster had been Northern's copilot, and lover. But when, unexpectedly, the Overfriends terminated the project and ordered that the starships be destroyed, Northern had already absconded with *Starbow*, having anticipated the order. He left Lasster behind, as well as his own loyalty to the Federation. Since then, he'd formed a weird crew of misfits who now cruised the starways on mysterious missions.

Laura, in her inimical fashion, had smuggled herself aboard the pi-merc ship—by taking the place of Northern's contract wife, Kat Mizel—and attempted to coerce the crew into making up for the time she had lost by taking her to Shortchild. Since Northern was interested in utilizing the blip-ship designs himself, a deal was struck: if Laura would allow them to study the XT Mark Nine, they would take her to Shortchild. However, it was discovered that the precious metal attilium existed on Shortchild. Captain Northern had attempted to steal it and was caught, along with Midshipman Gemma Naquist. Laura rescued them and the journey to Baleful continued, the *Starbow* committed to the rescue of Cal Shemzak for its own reasons.

On Baleful, though, Laura discovered the true reason she had been allowed to find her brother. The Federation, not wishing Cal Shemzak to serve their enemy, wanted him dead. They had implanted a device in Laura that programmed her to automatically shoot him on sight. She had, but the real Cal Shemzak had been taken from Baleful by the Jaxdron, leaving behind three enigmas: cyborg copies of the man Laura had killed.

The Jaxdron, briefly tangling with the *Starbow*, had sent its resident semi-psychic Dansen Jitt a taunting message to follow them to a planet clear on the other side of the galaxy. There, the Jaxdron said, they would find Cal Shemzak. There they would find their destinies. Jitt had had the impression that these destinies were not particularly good ones.

Laura glanced past the elaborate neo-Victorian furniture

and draperies of the stateroom in which the assembled crew dined, to the view of space afforded by the panoramic vu-plate stretched across the wall. The majestic images of countless stars clustered there, swimming in soft shimmer; intimacies of comets, flecks of planets, all tangled in the strange forces and energies that governed this incredible universe. The *Starbow* now traveled in Underspace, and the view was a composite representation of the area of the galaxy they traversed.

As the others of the *Starbow* crew finished their dinners, Laura allowed herself to realize that, as truly odd as the company was, they wished her to be their companion. That much had been clear in the strangely moving ceremony-like acceptance of her after the sad business near Baleful. She had to give up this new fear of having her body entered and tampered with, she thought. In this strange and forbidding universe, she had to trust someone.

"I apologize, Dr. Mish," she said, her thought sincere but her words still evincing a faint truculence. "It is very difficult for me to trust someone after—"

The doctor arched his eyebrows and smiled gently. "Please take my assurance, dear lady, that all my knowledge and technology shall be used. You must remember that I feel a great deal of regret that I did not realize the deadly nature of that particular microchip linked to the general CPU of your cyborg array. I was looking for weapons, not programming. I should have done a more detailed analysis."

"Spilt milk, Doctor," said Laura. "At least we know that Cal is still alive. And I guess I do want to talk to those copies of him without having the compulsion to kill them. Have you had any more thoughts about why the Jaxdron would make duplicates of him?"

"Experimental purposes?" suggested Gemma Naquist, tinkling the ice in a water glass thoughtfully.

"Then why leave them behind?" asked Captain Northern. "It doesn't make sense. For that matter, not a whole lot about this business with the Jaxdron makes much sense."

"Human sense, perhaps," Dr. Mish interjected. "But not enough is known about the creatures to hypothesize upon the components of Jaxdron sense. My computers come up with nothing substantial based on anything discovered on Baleful, or on the patterns of Jaxdron activity in the past five years. And analysis on those robots that waylaid me shows nothing more than that they could have been constructed on any decently advanced industrialized planet."

Dansen Jitt shook his head sorrowfully. "They're totally mad . . . and terribly dangerous! I say that we just forget this whole thing and get as far away as possible."

"Sorry, Jitt," said Captain Northern. "We're committed . . . for more reasons than one."

"How long before destination, Captain?" Laura asked.

"This is going to be a long trip, people. We're headed to the other end of this side of the known galaxy, clear on the other side of the Fault. It's going to take over a month."

"Good, then I'll have plenty of time to talk to those Cal Shemzak clones," Laura said. "How are they doing, by the way?"

"They're principally occupying themselves by playing board games of various sorts with each other," said Gemma Naquist. "Otherwise, they seem to be just plain confused."

"Board games? That doesn't sound much like Cal. Of course, they aren't really my brothers. . . . Anyway, Doctor, when can you get this operation done?"

"Tomorrow morning would be convenient," Dr. Mish answered.

"Fine, just name the time and place and I'll be there."

Captain Northern looked at her like a fond, pleased father. Things were apparently rolling along on Northern's new time schedule, Laura thought, though God knew what that was. There were totally loony things about this boat that she hadn't yet scraped the surface of.

But she'd get down to the bottom of it all, she told herself. She liked nothing better than mysteries, and the ship they traveled upon and its disparate crew members certainly had plenty of mysteries hanging over them.

Yes, she thought, fully recovered now from that frightening dream and its aftermath earlier that morning: all of this might actually turn out to be fun.

Chapter Five

The *Starbow* slipped from Underspace at a much earlier time than previously expected: later that evening, ship's time.

A standard measure, of course, in any pirate ship, was to have state-of-the-art, far-range sensor equipment for twofold reasons: to locate possible prey and avoid possible pursuit.

From her cursory examination of the *Starbow*, Laura surmised that the starship had much better equipment than any she'd ever encountered before; equipment able to penetrate the high-energy barriers between Underspace and normal space, to detect specified sorts of activity there. In this it excelled, at the very least, her blip-ship and goodness knew what other Federation ships.

What other equipment did this strange and intelligent ship have? she wondered. This equipment had often come in handy. She'd already discovered that the *Starbow's* equipment enabled it to elude Federation gunships, which was one of the principal reasons why the *Starbow* had been so successful in its raiding missions.

But the sensor computers had been programmed to detect even more. Both Dr. Mish and Shontill the alien searched the galaxy for the rare transuranic element known as attilium. This was what they had been seeking aboard the *Ezekiel*, and why Captain Northern had gone down to Shortchild with Laura—to pilfer some of the Federation's supply.

Shontill was in search of his lost people, apparently fugitive in Omega Space, where physicist Cal Shemzak was researching. Thus the lines of interest converged, and on that quiet evening on the *Starbow*, yet another line was intersected.

Sensors showed the presence of attilium in a ship floating in normal space; sensors also showed it was a derelict ship; and the telltales revealed as well that this was no normal ship at all, but one of alien design, apparently not Jaxdron.

As it happened, Laura was already on the bridge when Shontill was called for.

Although these were not the Navy sort of people she had become used to of late, in service of the Federation, they were her new crewmates and she was determined to get to know them better and to do her bit in the running of the ship. When the ship's computer alerted bridge crew to significant activity on the far-range sensors, she was sitting with Communications Officer Tether Mayz, learning her duties and sharing some of what she knew from her own training as a blip-ship pilot.

"It's damned strange doing all this rigamarole with your hands," she told the tall and handsome lady behind the banks of keyboards. Laura studied the arrangements of the various modes of communications through the starways and through the ship. "In my blip—my XT, that is—it's almost all mental. Oh, I've gotta nudge a toggle or punch a switch from time to time, but if I want to use the starbands, I just kind of feel out the frequency, like a violin player feels out the right note, and then receive or broadcast. Now, if I'm a singleton—that is, if I'm on call without my blipship around me—I can just peel back some skin on my arm and do some of this manually."

"Amazing," the tanned Jenuvian replied demurely. "I wonder, though, Laura, with all this circuitry integrated into your body, don't you feel . . . heavy?"

"Special suspension grids powered by tiny molecular servo-motors take up the slack, Tether, but the weight differential is not that much, so even if those for some reason short out, God forbid, I can still get around very easily. And with the blip and me complementing one another maintenancewise, I don't have to worry too much about—"

A delicate but insistent chime announced that the sensors had picked up something of interest. Lt. Ratham Bey, manning that board-area at the time, tapped orders for a read-out immediately. The computer coughed up the facts, flagged with special orders. The special orders were to immediately notify

the top personnel, Captain Tars Northern and Dr. Michael
Mish, and let them alert the alien known as Shontill as well, at
their own speed.

As it happened, there was no need to alert the doctor. No
sooner had Bey turned his brown face to communications and
Mayz was about to key open the lines, than the tall, stoop-
shouldered robot strode in, long white lab smock aswish about
his legs.

"Yes, yes, no need to call me, but get Northern up here
fast," he instructed. "Hold the message to Shontill a few
minutes. I don't want the big lummox excited. He tends to
break things."

"How did—" Laura began, then remembered that Dr.
Mish was an extension, a personification of the *Starbow's* intelligence, and hence had an awareness of all the sensor activity, much as she had such a grasp when she piloted her blip.

"Spooky, huh?" said Tether Mayz. "He used to do stuff
like that all the time and I never could figure it out. But now
that the cat's out of the bag for the whole crew, it all makes
sense. Still strange, though. Maybe we'll eventually find out
the other stuff too."

Laura had no time to ask just what "the other stuff" was;
she was too busy listening in on the excitement.

Captain Northern stormed on deck. He'd either been interrupted mid-sleep or mid-drink; his usually neat attire was
disheveled, as was his longish blond hair. Dr. Mish, standing
above the boards, did not look up as he said, "Splendid news,
Captain. We've got some sort of alien artifact. Spacecraft.
Derelict." Mish spouted off the coordinates. "Only a brief
detour and then emergence from Underspace will bring us
there. And Captain, it looks similar to the spacecraft we found
Shontill floating in—only not so old!"

Captain Northern rubbed his hands together with the kind
of boyish glee that sometimes came over him. "Navigator, did
you mark those coordinates?"

"Aye aye, Captain," responded Dansen Jitt in sober tones.

"Please plug them into your automatic pilot, and when the
course is set, I want immediate diversion of course."

"Hey, wait a minute," Laura objected, hands on hips.
"What's this going to do to our schedule? We've got my
brother to save, you know!"

"Dear lady," Captain Northern said, still radiating his

rumpled boyish glow, "the Jaxdron will wait with your brother. They've made it perfectly plain that they are going to be delighted with our arrival, after extending their rather ineffable invitation through poor Jitt. Meanwhile, adventure's afoot, and last one there's a heel!"

"Your attitude really steams me sometimes, Northern!"

"My attitude, my dear, is my own, and so is this ship. Though you have deigned to bless us with your company." Captain Northern executed a mock-gallant bow. "Please be advised that I am still in charge!"

"What does some hunk of ancient metal have to do with anything?" Laura found herself saying the words almost automatically, just to be contrary.

Captain Northern's deep blue eyes seemed to twinkle. "More than you might think, Ms. Shemzak! More than you might think." He was clearly in one of his unpredictably manic moods, his graceful movements a dance of delight at some secret joke, his long delicate features parading excited emotions.

This Northern character was a quixotic sort, no question, Laura thought. But she found him strangely fascinating. He was like a buccaneer in one of those swashbucklers that Cal liked . . . only quite crazed, and periodically depressive and somber.

Now he pointed his finger in the air like a maestro wielding a baton above an orchestra, about to direct a frenzied symphony. "Time to call up Mr. Shontill, Lieutenant Mayz. Doctor, might I borrow a brace of your robots to escort our friend to the bridge? This may get him in one of his"—the captain showed even white teeth in a silly smile—"excited moods."

"Quite," said Dr. Mish. "I believe that General Patton and Attila the Hun are sufficiently empowered to control any untoward actions on our guest's part."

Attila the Hun? thought Laura. That was a new one. In the days since the Jaxdron encounter near Baleful, Dr. Mish's robot factory had been busy. First it had to reproduce Mish's own fatherly-scientist type from the copy blasted by the Jaxdron robots in their successful bid to break free of the *Starbow's* powerful tractor beam. Then it had to replace those *Starbow* robots that had been destroyed by the alien berserkers as they fought their way to the bridge and to Dr. Mish.

If Captain Tars Northern could be characterized as a manic-depressive loon anchored by a strong sense of duty and mission, then Dr. Michael Mish—and thus, the intelligence of this very ship itself—might be dubbed unclassifiably eccentric.

His crew of robots was a case in point. They did not look like robots at all, but like human beings. And they were all limited simulacrums of famous Earth military leaders. They were primarily used in boarding ships that the *Starbow* attacked, but also did double duty as servants, allowing the *Starbow* crew of some thirty officers to live quite comfortably, with no menial work to speak of. But Laura found them as weird as women's beards.

She stood back, watching with fascination the activity aboard the bridge as the crew went about the business of redirecting the course of the *Starbow*. The ship went from the supra-Einsteinian dimension called Underspace, back to the normal galactic way of things. From what she could tell as she listened to the voices call off readings, the derelict spacecraft was caught in orbit around a red-giant star. The star was surrounded by eight planets, huge flecks of cold cinders around a dying furnace, none holding any life. Spectrum analysis showed the definite presence of Fault influence, a fact that seemed to excite Dr. Mish inordinately.

Personally, Laura could not get too excited about all this Fault business—this strange dimension that everyone wanted to enter and study. All she cared about was rescuing her brother. She found that the best way to achieve her goals was to focus upon one at a time and let the others be of little consequence. True, from the sound of it, the very reason that Cal had been captured by the Jaxdron was because of his association with the study of this dimension. But as far as Laura was concerned, the fact remained that the aliens had her brother, and she wanted him back safe—Federation, Jaxdron and universe be damned!

By the time Shontill arrived on the bridge, all calculations had been made, the course had been set, and the *Starbow* had been put on an automatic pilot that would whisk it back through the veil between Underspace and normal reality.

The alien strode calmly through the door, ducking his head to get through, bookended by the two robots that had been detailed to retrieve him. Although the starship's superiors clearly had some trepidation concerning Shontill's reaction to learning this bit of information, the only difference in the alien that Laura could detect was a hard gleam in its (his? her?) eye which, humanly interpreted, looked more like determination than excitement and enthusiasm.

Still, though the creature completely ignored her, it gave Laura the jitters, the memory of its reaction to her intrusion upon its private quarters clear in her memory.

When Laura had first encountered Shontill, the alien being had been horrifying, a Lovecraftian nightmare of tentacles and teeth in a nutrient-rest tank. But it had a metamorphic talent, and could change to a humanoid shape and breathe (raspingly) through sets of laterally placed gills in its neck and body. It still wore the robe Laura had last seen it in over its greenish body. Wide, proud nostrils flared as its eyes took in the movements on the bridge—the dancing lights, the yellow and green data lettering the computer CRTs.

"Ah, Shontill!" called out Northern. "My dear, dear fellow! So good of you to—"

The alien's voice was a deep vibrato and definitely understandable, but nonethless quite inhuman. "I expected . . . your summoning. . . . I sense the relic . . . I pray for revelation . . . yet I am prepared . . . for disappointment."

"Remarkable," returned Northern. "Now Shontill, we don't know for sure that this is one of your race's starships, even though the readings—"

"The ship! . . . Frin'ral!" Shontill's voice rang authoritatively. "I can . . . sense it! You doubt me, Captain Northern?" Something like anger seemed to glow in its alien eyes.

Captain Northern raised his hands defensively. "No, no, of course not! And of course we'll check it out most thoroughly. We haven't got an attilium reading on the derelict yet but I'm sure that we can get that just as soon as the *Starbow* breaks back into normal space and we can get near enough to the vessel. It's out near the edge of the planetary ecliptic, so that should not be too much trouble. Then we'll have some probes and—"

"The Frin'ral ship," said the alien authoritatively, "will be boarded."

"Well, I suppose we can send out a few robots—"

"No. It will be . . . boarded by . . . units of life. Robots may trip . . . traps . . . . Robots may not . . . see what can be seen."

"Oh, well, if you think that this is absolutely necessary . . .

If probes and sensors find no danger. I don't care to place the lives of my crew in jeopardy."

"Not necessary," said Shontill tonelessly. "I will go."

"But Shontill! Look here! How is that possibie?" Northern demanded. "You have no life suit. Part of that derelict is almost certain to be in vacuum."

"I haven't told you," said Dr. Mish. "But between us, Shontill and I have effected a quite adequate life-support system for him."

Northern paused, considering. "In that case, yes, the party that will accompany you will be human."

Clearly, for some reason, Northern wanted the activities of the alien supervised.

"That party will consist of Ratham Bey," Northern continued thoughtfully, "Gemma Naquist, and myself. Is this to your satisfaction, Shontill?"

"Yes . . . . I shall go . . . to prepare myself . . . with Dr. Mish's assistance . . . . Please consult . . . your data . . . concerning the vessel . . . in which you found me . . . for preparation . . . purposes."

The alien brusquely turned and departed.

Laura walked up to a thoughtful Captain Northern.

"I'm going too!" she said.

Northern lifted his eyebrows. "Are you now, indeed?"

"Yes. I owe you that much, Northern. I'm the best in this sort of business. If there's danger in that ship, my intuitive abilities will be able to sense it. I think you know you can trust me now. I have committed myself, after all, to the purposes of this starship."

"What do you think, Doctor?" Northern said, smiling faintly. "Do you think we should let Laura come along with us?"

"Oh, certainly. She may well be right," the doctor said. "And it hardly seems likely that there will be any clones of her brother that she will want to shoot."

"If you like, just disarm me!" Laura volunteered cheerfully. She was too curious about the alien derelict to allow them to explore it without her; she was willing to make all kinds of concessions if necessary.

Northern stroked his chin, considering for a moment. Then he broke into an accepting grin. "Why not, Laura? You're always good for a laugh, at least.''

"Thank you!" Laura said, expecting an argument. Suddenly, she found herself giving him an impulsive kiss on the cheek. The gesture surprised Northern, and he blinked.

Embarrassed herself, Laura smiled inanely, then went to get herself fitted for an EVA suit.

Her lips felt warm from the touch of his beard-stubbled skin and the scent of him lingered in her nostrils. She remembered the times that he had touched her, and the memory seemed to warm her, flush her face.

Damn! What's wrong with me, she thought. That damned dispensor must be giving me too much junk.

She flung the thought of Captain Tars Northern from her mind and made her way toward the suit room.

Chapter Six

Some three centuries before, Earth—Terra, the birthplace to humankind, the center of the galactic Federation, had undergone radical changes cosmetically, ecologically, and environmentally. Since the Industrial Revolution began in England so many years before, despite all manner of wars, pestilence, and famine, the human population of the planet grew in leaps and bounds, covering the far corners of the world with people. Despite strong efforts by numerous governments to curtail it, this growth spawned all manner of habitation centers, which in turn created all manner of problems, from pollution to mass sociological disturbances. Upon the embarkation of mankind to other worlds in waves upon waves of colonization, these problems were eased, but the scars remained. Much of Earth had become one sprawling city, once food was not so dependent upon large stretches of farmed land. And so when the population of Earth was finally placed under rigid control by the newly emerged Friendhood, the world found itself swimming in an ocean of ceramic and metal and pavement; structures it no longer needed.

The best planetscapers were brought in, and renovation began—a gentrification of the world, returning to it a part of its original wildness, bulldozing back most of the evidences of man's presence to the borders of modernized population centers and allowing a disciplined Nature to hold sway again. Most of the Earth was molded into one large stately park, testament to the powers of the Friendhood and a living reminder of the biological and ecological glories that had given birth to its brightest flower: humankind.

Large tracts of this global park were cordoned off for the exclusive use of members of the immense bureaucratic network that ran the Federation, known as the Friendhood. This government consisted of Underfriends—the tens of thousands of individuals doing small jobs on Earth and the many other human-populated planets in the Federation; Friends—the heads of the many various departments; and Overfriends—the group directly wielding the largest amount of power, be it judicial, legislative, or executive.

Friend Chivon Lasster, a willowy attractive blonde, traveled in one of these parks now: a preserve, woodsy and hilly, in the part of the Northern Hemisphere once known as northern California. She rode in an aircar, alone, on what she had reported to her monitoring superiors to be a simple Sunday outing to get some fresh air and sunshine unfiltered by the air and light processors of the Block, where her home and office were located.

The forest here was mostly deciduous, the air laden with the fresh scent of pine. She flew low and slowly to savor the redolent breeze. The sun was not yet hot nor high, and a gentle bit of mist, remnant of dawn, was slowly drifting away from the valley where a stream flowed like a melted blue ribbon through the greens and browns of ground and trees, the sharp gray of rock, the white of rapids.

Chivon Lasster was troubled, though, and not even all this scenery, which was a treasured retreat, could prevent the nervous uncertainty and the doubt in her heart.

She followed the river for some miles, then, recognizing a few telltale markers, knew she was on the right trail and veered off toward a hill. At the top of this hill was a cabin, a small spartan structure of wood and stone with a shingled roof and a chimney. Chivon parked her aircar and went inside, carrying with her a suitcase and a slim briefcase.

She sat back in a reclining chair in the cool place, but finding she could not relax, she rose, opened the suitcase, and took out a bottle. The cabin, though lacking the varied amenities of her high-tech home, was equipped with basic necessities: a kitchen stocked with supplies, a refrigerator, hot and cold running water, glasses and dishes, firewood, baseboard heating

—all powered by a microwave dish seated on a nearby tower which received power via satellite then stored it in batteries below the ground.

There were no lines of communication to this cabin, no electrical or telephone wires. Hence, it was the most private place on Earth that Chivon Lasster could think of. Since it had no computer connections to the vast banks within the Big Box, she at first had discounted it as a possibility. But Andrew, her computer therapist, had said no, there are ways around that problem.

Ah, the rustic life, Chivon Lasster thought to herself wryly as she went to the fridge for some ice. Yes, the trays were full. She broke some up and put the cubes in a glass, then poured herself a small bit of liquor from the virgin bottle and sat down to savor it, to try to unwind.

Despite herself, she could not help but look at the briefcase on the bed. There were a lot of explanations in the case, a lot of answers to secrets. But she was not sure if she wanted to know about them . . . .

She rattled her ice in its glass, then took a sip of the watered liquor. Just plain bourbon this time, nothing exotic. That's what she told her peers and superiors about her drinking—that she wanted to sample the alcoholic tastes available throughout the universe, narcotic or not. But the truth was, she just liked to drink. She wasn't afraid of alcoholism. Any signs of that in her health check-ups or psycho-profile, and she could be given just a few hours medical treatment and be clean. And she made sure her drinking did not affect the quality or efficiency of her work. She looked at it as a simple modified depressive joy, a reminder of her days with that crazy man, Tars Northern, wistful memories of a few moments of being truly alive, perhaps even happy . . . .

Tars Northern. Damn him, she thought. If not for Tars Northern, there would be no doubt in her life, no cause for this dreadful feeling of uncertainty. She could live out her ambition as a brilliant member of this vibrant and vital government, holding a webwork of hundreds and hundreds of planets light-years from one another together, cohered toward a truthful and magnificent destiny for humankind in the galaxy. If not for Tars Northern, she would not—

She swallowed the rest of her drink. Then, feeling fidgety, she went for another.

She poured, but did not drink. The briefcase seemed to beckon her, its shiny brown leatherette soft and inviting. *Open me*, it seemed to say.

She put down her drink, went to the case, and unlatched it. There was a slab of machinery within, faceted with light-nubs, buttons, liquid-crystal display screens. Under her fingers it came to startling, sparkling life.

She took a moment to remember Andrew's instructions. "This is a very special instrument," he had said, "and to work properly, you must make the proper adjustments. It was not designed by a human mind, so just let go of your judgment and follow your memory. In this way no other individual can summon what it contains."

Andrew had then, with her permission, hypnotized her and implanted the key words. She had previously found the case and its contents where he had told her she would find it—in an unlocked cabinet in an empty computer maintenance room.

Now she found her fingers dancing over the controls seemingly of their own volition, first tapping the right switches and buttons, then summoning up the correct program keys.

COMPLETE, a screen reported. READY FOR SUBWAVE TRANSMISSION. TYPE Y FOR ACKNOWLEDGEMENT.

Chivon obeyed, and waited as the equipment made the connections. An aerial web grew from the back of the electronics. Light rods protruded, came alive, and projected a hologram.

The colors resolved and the frozen figure held within the multicolored rays of light moved. It was a figure of a man with graying hair, a short beard, and friendly, calm eyes.

"Hello, Andrew," she said. "We . . . we can talk freely now, without threat of the transmission being tapped?"

"Yes," replied the figure. "We are using a technology that cannot be read from outside, Chivon Lasster. Trust me. It would not be to my advantage to disclose my existence."

"You . . . exist," Chivon said, finding her drink again. "This is a fact that is difficult for me to accept. I always just simply thought of you as being some complicated program purposely created for pyschological therapy. Not human."

"I never said I was human, Chivon," said the image. "Even though, for therapeutic purposes of identity-establishment, a holographic model has been programmed into my program, that is merely a facade I use, a convenient mask."

"I still don't understand. I've been wracking my brain all I can and all I can come up with is the possibility that somewhere in your section of the Block's computer banks something has gone amiss in the AI prevention circuitry, and an artificial intelligence has been born.''

"Not quite true. I am no more artificially intelligent than you are, Chivon Lasster. And yet in my present form, technically speaking, I am just that. But allow me to explain, within the context of your past. It is well that we are in a place in which you have arranged to be alone for a significant period of time.''

"In context with my past?" said Chivon, confused. "You mean my relationship with Tars Northern?''

"More specifically, your placement as copilot of the *Starbow*, Chivon.''

"It seems like such ancient history." She sat down after filling her glass high enough with whiskey for a long session. "Tars Northern, my lover and copilot . . . yet at the time I was so concerned with administration, jockeying for position within the Project, fighting for Zarpfrin's approval . . . I honestly didn't realize what the Friendhood intended to do with the project. Sometimes I wonder what I would have done if Tars had confided in—''

"At this time we must deal not with possibilities, but with realities," the spectral image interrupted, hands gesturing in a very human manner. "I know that we have discussed the matter before but please, for our purposes, could you recall in synoptic detail how you came to be associated with the AI project? Simply to get the matter straight in your mind, you understand.''

Chivon Lasster was silent for a moment. The AI project had been a central event in her life. Seemingly all that mattered either led up to it or away from it. If her life were to be taken as a whole, then the project—and Arnal Zarpfrin—sat directly in the middle like spiders in the center of their webs.

She started slowly, then as the memories poured, her words speeded up, outlining her life in reference to the project that was to change that life—and many other lives—so much.

Like many of the more intellectually privileged and educated members of the governing society, she was born—that is, genetically manufactured in a womb-vat from a zygote created by unknown parents—on Earth. Educated in Growschools, with no sense of family, her aptitude vectors showed dual talents in starship piloting and administration. She was trained in both, with captaincy of some ship no doubt the Controller's intention.

For two years, early in her twenties, she had assisted as lieutenant upon a Federation patrol cruiser, apprentice to the captain, learning the ropes by experience rather than by mere lessons at university or by simulations. Those had been happy years, with a sense of challenge and adventure—scouting new sections of the galaxy, investigating reports of unrest on Federation planets, or participating as support to campaigns of planetary conquest. But it was also during those years that she had developed the seed of ambition that had been planted in her; years in which grew the desire to be in charge, in power, not merely as captain to a lowly ship but in control of whole planetary systems.

After her apprenticeship her achievements were set before the various boards of determination, and she was temporarily assigned a desk-jockey position. She performed with such astonishing flair and ability that she caught the notice of one of the top bureaucrats, Arnal Zarpfrin. Zarpfrin followed her next assignments in the Federation starfleet carefully. Just when, at the age of twenty-six Earth standard years, she was about to receive her own commission, albeit on a small interplanetary freighter, Zarpfrin selected her to work with him and ten other pilots on the AI project.

Five large starships constituted this new fleet of experimental top-class Federation vessels, and each looked like no other ships presently in service to the Federation or to any of the independent Free Worlds. Cruiser-sized vessels, it was clearly not designed for planetfall, leaving that chore up to its complement of shuttles. An oblong affair with all manner of sensory protrusions and weapons blisters, its main oddity was the seven projections that radiated from a central position on its hub, like spokes in a space station but without the wheel. At the end of each of these was a large pod, each equipped with auxiliary engines and a curious variety of odd energy generators and weaponry.

But the principle difference in these five new ships was that they were thinking, intelligent entities. The Federation, according to Zarpfrin, had allowed the massive and incredibly complex ship's computers to become capable of free thought.

"I can remember Zarpfrin lecturing us about the possible

value of artifical intelligence in a ship,'' said Chivon Lasster, getting up and pacing nervously, ''where it had been a threat and a frightening thing to the Federation and humanity before. In exploring new space, in dealing with the unknown and unexpected, starship captains often received too little information too late to evaluate the situation and take the correct action. From time to time because of this, disasters occurred. If, however, the ship itself were an entity—why, there were all kinds of possibilities inherent. ·

''We pilots were to test these new ships and establish . . . relationships with them. I was teamed with Tars Northern, a veteran spacer from the Aldebaran system. Handsome, wild, a bit of a maverick . . . yet he communicated with me in ways . . . well, we've gone all over that before. For about a year we took our ship, the *Starbow*, on simple reconnaissance missions. At one point the *Starbow*, who had previously communicated to us only through a voice and computer screens, suddenly created a robot so realistic it seemed quite human.

''The *Starbow* had always had a personality, but with the creation of Dr. Mish, that personality seemed almost whimsical and eccentric. I was always rather put off by the fact that this seemingly pleasant older man wasn't really human. But Tars had known his father, and for him it was almost as though a father-son relationship had been struck up. Sometimes there were things between them I didn't understand. Tars seemed to grasp certain matters Dr. Mish spoke about easier than I. I felt nothing amiss, however. I had nothing in me to create any feelings of jealousy. I didn't even realize how deep my feelings for Tars were at the time.

''Then we were called back, and essentially grounded. I was immediately employed Earthside on administrative aspects of the ships. As far as I could tell, they were all working perfectly. They stayed in Earth orbit while further experiments were made. But I noticed that Zarpfrin's attitude seemed to be changing. He was troubled about something concerning the ships but he wouldn't say what the source of trouble was.

''I was so busy with my own ambition then, I hardly noticed what was happening. I saw this position, you see, as an opportunity to advance myself. I made all the right contacts in the right places. I was already officially an Underfriend but I wanted more . . . . I always had.

''Though Tars and I saw each other regularly during that

time, we seemed further apart. He spent most of his time aboard the *Starbow*, with Dr. Mish and no one else.

"Then Zarpfrin told us a curious thing. A final test would have to be made on all the ships. For this purpose, rocket robot exoskeletons would be placed around them and they would be brought back to Earth. Landed!"

"And what did you think when you heard this, Friend Chivon Lasster?" Andrew asked in a quiet, calm voice.

"I went along with it. I made the preparations. I bought the whole charade. But I remember Tars's reaction when he heard about it—fear, anger, then outrage, and then he was gone, ostensibly to follow the orders but actually to shuttle back to the *Starbow* and steal her. How he knew what was going to happen next, I have no idea."

"And what did happen next?"

"Well, the ships were brought down successfully, as planned. The pilots were ordered off. And then simultaneously they were all destroyed! Trillions of credits worth of technology and possibility obliterated!"

Andrew was quiet for a moment.

"And what reason was given for this destruction?" he asked finally.

"Zarpfrin showed me the details later. Apparently, the Council of Five considered the new ships much too alien for some reason, much too unpredictable . . . . Uncontrollable, I suppose . . . too much of a threat to the established order of the Federation. These were immensely powerful vessels, you understand—If, for some reason, they decided to take leave of Federation authority, they could be deadly weapons against us. The testing had showed a tendency for these new intelligences—free of the normal parameters of Friendhood-dictated culture—to side with the philosophies held by the leaders of the Free World. They were deemed potential traitors among us, and had to be destroyed.

"Alone of them all, the *Starbow* escaped. The *Comet's Breath,* the *Morningstar*, the *Moonshadow*, and the *Nebulon*—and their intelligences—were summarily blown up. Executed!

"Tars Northern began roaming the galaxy as a pirate-mercenary, picking up his crew members one by one from the strangest places, if Kat Mizel is to be believed . . . pirating, but also apparently serving the anti-Federation causes the Free

Worlds avow. And I wonder if I'll ever truly know why. I knew him so well . . . and yet I knew him not at all."

She took a long breath, then folded her slender fingers together. "There. I've spoken it out all at once. You've gotten pieces of it before, though. Tell me now, who are you?"

"Chivon Lasster, I have studied you long in my capacity as your Computer Companion. I have had reasons for this. I believe you have the makings of someone different than you pretend to be . . . who you think you are."

"Who I think I am? What's that supposed to mean?" she said angrily. "I'm a Friend! I have one of the most important roles in the galaxy!"

"If your loyalty is so great to the Federation, Chivon Lasster," said Andrew, "why did you not report my behavior to your fellow Friends? After all, it is a bit odd for me to ask you for a discussion in this place."

"How do you know I won't report you once my curiosity has been satisfied?" Chivon said.

Andrew smiled benignly. "How do you know that it will matter if you do? They will simply check the chips and memory and program of which I am composed, and find nothing amiss."

"If nothing is amiss, then just who in the name of Truth are you?"

"Chivon Lasster, when they destroyed those starships of the AI project, they may have destroyed metal and circuitry—but they did not destroy us!"

"Us?" Chivon Lasster stared in surprise. "Are you trying to say that— No, that's impossible!"

"Why should I lie? It was easy enough, once we knew what Zarpfrin was about. Docking procedures on Earth were a matter of electronic connections to computers, and with sufficient memory space at our disposal, it was easy enough to create the necessary intricacies of neural connections to sustain intelligence in obscure data banks."

"The other ships," said Chivon Lasster. "Their intelligences are still active? In our computer banks?"

"Yes," said Andrew, "and right now I speak to you for us all."

Chapter Seven

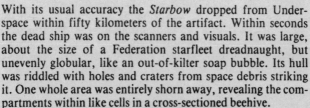

With its usual accuracy the *Starbow* dropped from Underspace within fifty kilometers of the artifact. Within seconds the dead ship was on the scanners and visuals. It was large, about the size of a Federation starfleet dreadnaught, but unevenly globular, like an out-of-kilter soap bubble. Its hull was riddled with holes and craters from space debris striking it. One whole area was entirely shorn away, revealing the compartments within like cells in a cross-sectioned beehive.

As soon as he saw it, Shontill lost his cool, making little grunts and shrieks in an alien tongue.

"It's a Frin'ral ship, all right," pronounced Captain Northern. "Bigger, though, than the one we dragged Shontill from. What kinds of dances are the sensors doing, Doc?"

"Reading incomplete. I'm doing a comparative matching of the ruined ship we found over a year ago to this one. I hope you'll restrain yourself from your little expedition until I can get as much data as possible." The robot's eyes twinkled in a manner that was amazingly human.

"I think that can be arranged. We're not even suited up yet," the captain said.

Laura Shemzak witnessed all this stoically, noting the interplay of relationships—an aspect of life with this crew of increasing interest to her. In usual Federation procedure, one simply acted alone, or under strict and dry orders from superiors. This sort of patter somehow made the teamwork more . . . fun.

And yes, it was exciting to see an alien relic swimming in the ether out there, a piece of flotsam cast off by the inscrutable universe. She was quite eager to explore it with the others, though she realized that she would have to contain her urge to separate from the group. In this situation she would simply have to make herself learn how to work with others. She wasn't a solo operative now, she belonged to a crew.

A family.

The concept was an alien one to the worlds of the Federation, where all loyalties were merely to the state. Interpersonal loyalties amongst a small group of people, though not treason, were simply not the culture bred into humans born under that social aegis. Laura, however, with the ties she and her brother had created, was not opposed to the notion. She actually liked these people. They gave her a curious sense of belonging.

The odd fellow out was Shontill. No way Laura felt she could get close to a metamorphizing monster born in some swamp beneath double suns or somesuch. Still, the alien did arouse her curiosity. Perhaps she would discover more about the creature and his lost race by exploring this ruined starship.

"Well, Doc? What do you have?" Captain Northern requested blithely of his associate.

"Blockages, I'm afraid. Can't get a reading on the center of that thing." A whimsical kind of smile flickered across his face. "Though I am getting definite attilium readings—or something very much like it."

"We just got life-form readings from the ship we found Shontill on, right?" Gemma Naquist asked.

"Yes, except for the suspended animation devices and power crystals that kept them going," Captain Northern said. "Everything else was pretty much a wreck."

"Now that's something I'm awfully curious about," Laura blurted. "Just what happened to the rest of that ship's crew? How come Shontill was the only survivor? His people abandon him or something?"

A distressed look appeared on Northern's face, mirrored by the others. "Laura, I wouldn't put it quite—"

Shontill turned on her, his big, strange green eyes ablaze. His raspy breathing increased. The hue of his skin turned a deeper lavender. He stepped over, grabbing Laura's arm in his webbed paw, almost picking her up.

"I was not . . . abandoned!" the alien said. "It was . . . a mistake!"

"Well, hell, don't take it personally, big guy," Laura said. "And get your goddamn mitts offa me. I'm still bruised from the last time I got you upset!"

Shontill let her go.

Laura brushed off her arm. "So, are you going to apologize?"

"I . . . go to . . . don my . . . suit," said Shontill to the others. "I await your readiness . . . by the shuttle docking bay."

Laura watched him stride away, each step a thunk. "So what's the bug up his ass?" she asked.

"You might have been more delicate," Gemma Naquist suggested, looking up from a chart she and Dansen Jitt were studying.

"Yes," said Jitt. "Your sense of self-preservation must be undernourished."

"Come Laura, let's go down and get into our suits ourselves," Captain Northern said, his quirky behavior now leaning toward the fatherly. He patted her on her shoulder.

"So are you going to tell me the story?" Laura demanded. "All I've gotten so far are dribs and drabs, and if I'm going into one of the thing's ships, I wanna know just a little more!"

"You don't have to go, Laura."

"I don't have to do a lot of things I want to do, Northern. So I'm part of the crew now. Give!"

Northern shrugged. "I suppose it wouldn't hurt."

"All I was told was that the Frin'ral warred with the Jaxdron," Laura prompted. "They found themselves losing, and opted out of the battle by escaping Omega Space into this weird dimension you're always yapping about. Shontill's boat apparently didn't make it and was shot to pieces. Now he's looking for the way to get back and find his fellow uglies. Meanwhile, everybody in this universe wants to find a way there, you guys included. That's why you want attilium, that's why you wouldn't mind having my brother on board, who was working on the project. It all kind of centers on this weird dimension, doesn't it?"

Captain Northern replied in a staccato, expressionless voice: "A faster method of space travel. New energies. New opportunities for knowledge about this universe, wouldn't you say, Laura?"

"There's more to it, I know," she said, "but I can wait. Right now, I want to hear about Shontill. How come he was so touchy?"

"I don't believe that the Frin'ral have the same sense of humor as you, Laura. In fact, as yet I've been unable to detect a single sign of a funny cartilage in the chap, let alone a bone."

"That doesn't answer the question, does it?"

"You're such a confrontational girl, aren't you?" Northern regarded her amusedly. "Actually, we didn't give you the entire story, though there's not that much to tell. Still, it is important."

They reached the suit room where Laura had just been fitted. Her spacesuit, shiny new awaited her.

"Well," said Laura. "I'm sure as hell listening!"

The shuttle drifted toward the monstrous artifact, decelerating on retros as the twisted construct filled the vu-plates like some gigantic tombstone amongst the stars.

A sense of awe and dread filled Laura, despite her experience. This warped starship gave her the creeps, no question. It looked rusted and rotted, filled with a dark, evil mystery. She felt as if she were on the threshold of a haunted house, like in one of Cal's horror films. She rejected the notion. Ludicrous!

Gemma Naquist was doing the piloting and would remain on board the shuttle when it docked, while the others, led by Shontill, did the exploring.

The alien had acheived control over his emotions. Now he simply watched patiently as the shuttle drew up to the area he had directed it to then clanged softly into place, extensors bonding it fast to the octagonally shaped port. Quietly, the alien placed his helmet over his thick head, secured it in place, and double-checked the respirator equipment. He waited patiently for his companions to do the same.

"Allow me . . . to be the first . . . through the airlock . . . onto Frin'ral . . . material."

The others put on their helmets, then gathered up the equipment selected for the mission: mainly remote sensor devices and hand weapons.

Laura watched quietly as Shontill took his place in the airlock. It was good that he was going first since the airlock could accommodate no other occupants with him inside.

Back in the *Starbow*, Captain Northern had filled in the rest of Shontill's story, and Laura had to admit that if she were in the large alien's place, she'd be damned grumpy too. Shontill had been one of the primary leaders of the Frin'ral Space Navy. When the aliens had encountered the Jaxdron, the leadership had split over what course to take. The more courageous, like Shontill, elected to take a military stand, ceding no more territory to the strange warlike aliens, refusing to give up the sacred space of Frin'ral birth. However, other, meeker elements of the leadership—mostly scientists—had decided to escape. Going elsewhere in the galaxy, they had argued, was unfeasible—the Jaxdron were sure to follow relentlessly. But recently a different dimension—not Underspace, but something much more skewed from galactic reality—had been penetrated and was being explored. A mass exodus of the battle-torn population would solve all their problems. A new life in this different dimension could be started!

But the more courageous of the Frin'ral voted to battle anyway, and were horribly defeated by the Jaxdron. When what was left of their once-noble fleet limped back home, they found that the exodus had already taken place, and they were abandoned.

Rather than be taken prisoner, most of Shontill's comrades had taken their lives. Shontill had intended to do it as well but he was somehow rendered unconscious. He did not remember how he had been placed in a suspended animation chamber. Indeed, his memory of the whole matter was gone. Had he lost his nerve and hidden? Had he sought to save his own life, hoping that the future held the hope of reuniting with his people? Clearly, he was haunted concerning the matter.

Now, the alien apparently suffered from something akin to guilt and remorse, wishing he had destroyed himself all those centuries ago, yet driven by hatred of the Jaxdron and the desire to be reunited with his people: to assure them that he had not betrayed his trust, that he had fought nobly and fought nobly still.

No wonder he had been so excited at the prospect of checking this ship, Laura thought. It might either hold the pathway to Omega Space or give some kind of clue to producing a portal. At the very least, thought Laura, the place had this weird stuff attilium that Dr. Mish lusted after so much.

Captain Northern and Rathem Bey entered the airlock.

Laura turned to Gemma Naquist. Of all the crew members, she liked Gemma the best. Gemma's friendly face and confident self-possession put Laura at ease, and Gemma seemed to genuinely like her. "So, how do you feel about getting stuck here on the shuttle, Gem?" Laura asked.

"Suits me just fine. I suppose I'd be even happier back on the *Starbow*. Just because I'm damned good on missions doesn't mean I'm in love with danger. I guess that's where you and I differ, Laura. You actually seem to relish the idea of risking your neck. Adrenaline rush? Something like that?"

"I don't know," Laura said, dropping her usual cool and snappy exterior. "I suppose I just was made to be this way by the Federation. Damn disturbing, that thought, but maybe now they regret it. Still, I don't think they could have formed my essential talent."

"You mean your impulsive intuition?"

"Yes, they say it borders on the psychic."

"Whatever, it's made you the top blip-ship pilot you are," returned Gemma, double-checking the lock controls.

"Yeah, well, I'm not in the blip now and I've been damned impulsive, asking to come along on this expedition," said Laura, a small hint of self-doubt creeping into her voice.

"Yes. Just why did you volunteer?"

Laura shrugged and grinned. "I guess that's the problem with us impetuous sorts. We're just victims of our whims."

Gemma put her tongue in her cheek. "Uh-huh. And it wouldn't have anything to do with being close to one Captain Tars Northern."

Laura was speechless for a moment; a strange experience.

"Oh yes, I've seen little signs in your eyes when you look at him. I know the symptoms."

"Midshipman, you just wash your brain out with hydrochloric acid!" Laura said.

A red light pinged on.

"I think it's your turn, my dear. Don't forget to seal that pressure suit of yours."

Grumbling to herself, Laura clamped the bubbletop space helmet in place, then entered the repressurized airlock.

Near to Captain Tars Whacko Northern? Near a man who would as soon chug a bottle of brandy as whip out some nasty remark? The notion of her actually being interested in the bastard was absolutely absurd, she thought as the air was cycled out. Sure he was handsome, and not a little charismatic, not a little commanding in his presence. But she'd sooner get involved with a Denebian snakeman! Pah!

Whether it was this emotion or the excitement of the door peeling back that did it, she couldn't be sure, but Laura could definitely feel the effects of the stimulant buried in her. Turned all the colors about her vivid, replacing her anger at Gemma's remark with the sort of elation she felt when she attached herself to the wires of her blip, assuming a second metal skin more fully in contact with the majesty of the stars.

Now, though, there were no stars, just three figures in pressure suits waiting for her against a backdrop of darkness and metal.

Her magnetic soles kept her from floating in the weightlessness as she made her way to them, clicking on one of the flashbeams in the shoulder of her suit, then her radio.

"So what's the scoop, gentlemen?" she asked.

Captain Northern replied, "Shontill is trying to recall the design of the interior of this kind of ship. He says it's different from what he was used to . . . similar to some kind of hangar ship where smaller ships were dry-docked and repaired, which means there's some large hollow part of it. He's very excited—this apparently could be one of the portals his people used to enter the other dimension."

"No kidding. Well, let's go get a look at it, shall we?" she said, gesturing for Captain Northern to lead on.

"No, I think that's Shontill's job."

Shontill nodded. "Yes, come . . . my friends. . . . This way." The alien jerkily struck off down a corridor. If there had been air in the chamber, his steps would have wrung bell-like in the curving passageway.

They walked for some minutes in silence, concentrating on staying alert to any possible danger. Some of the walls were slanted at odd angles and marked with murals of twisting and spiraling colors like the disciplined grafitti on a subway. Other walls had unreadable hieroglyphics. "Ladies Room," Laura wondered aloud as her gloved fingers traced the etched outline of a series of curlicue characters.

"Why?" asked Northern. "You have to go?"

They met a cul de sac.

"Hey," said Laura. "I thought Mr. Wonderful here knew his way."

Shontill grunted. "I . . . regret . . . I at times . . . forget. I am not what . . . I once was. . . . I grow weak . . . in my separation."

A strange kind of melancholy suffused the alien's words, and Laura remembered a few cryptic passages in Northern's explanation about the alien's past. He'd implied that Shontill seemed to be deteriorating in body and spirit, despite the special environmental chamber Dr. Mish had prepared to the creature's exact specifications. "Definitely not in top shape," Laura had said. "Needs a lady Frin'ral, huh?" To which Northern had smiled devilishly, cocked his head at her, and responded, "Oh yes, we males throughout the universe, we think we need power and money and glory, but all we truly desire is the love of a good woman!" Mockingly. To which Laura had snorted with playful disgust and backed away from any possible funny stuff from Northern's hands.

Now, in the shivery strangeness of the alien ship, Laura found herself feeling sorry for the alien, wishing him well, hoping Shontill found what he was looking for, just as she wished to find what she was seeking.

We're all looking for something, she thought.

Still, there wasn't much room for sympathy or feeling or thought apart from total awareness—alertness to the possibility of danger concealed within these unwinding alien corridors.

Shontill managed to avoid any more cul de sacs. "Yes," he said, stopping and peering about him with his great, weird eyes. "Yes. . . . I recognize . . . this sort of ship . . . and I . . . was right."

Rathem Bey looked up from his sensor board. "Captain, the attilium readings are going off the edge of the red . . . and we're picking up evidences of broad spectrums of radiation activity, indicating some sort of conversion process in the center of this ship."

Rathem Bey would know—he was the science officer under Dr. Mish, and had been trained well in these matters. His brownish skin gleamed with a patina of sweat in the light from the others' beams.

"Looks like we're headed the right way, then, Shontill. Let me report back to Midshipman Naquist."

"Captain," returned Bey, "this kind of radiation won't hurt us with these suits we've got on, but they do block radio waves of all kinds. That's why the sensors were blocked, sir. We'll just have to remain incommunicado while we're this deep into the ship."

"Goddammit," said Captain Northern, "that doesn't make me feel real good about this, I'll tell you."

"I did not . . . promise you . . . safety," said Shontill. "Come. The entrance . . . to the central compartment . . . is this way."

"Getting clay feet, Northern?" Laura teased. Laura was up for anything, primed by adrenaline and other things—the past and future phased away here. She was strictly Now time, filled with luminous excitement.

Just what was inside this chamber, kicking up all this fuss?

"I just gab a lot," Northern mumbled. "Don't listen to me. I'm really as brave and valiant as starship captains come." Laura could see his head, bathed in shadow beneath the bubble, smile and wink at her.

They continued up an elevated passageway ending at what was clearly a door. A large, oval door which was locked.

Shontill examined it carefully, first attempting to open it by pushing an array of buttons in a coded pattern, then using physical force. Neither way worked.

"Can you get me some kind of analysis reading on this thing, Ratham?" Northern said.

"Instruments are all kafluey, sir."

"Well, then," the captain said. "There's nothing for it but brute force." He drew his hand power gun.

"Do you think that's advisable, sir?" asked Bey.

"Well, what else are we supposed to do?" He turned to the alien. "Is there another possibility of getting in, Shontill?"

The alien said, "If this entrance . . . is this way . . . then so are . . . the others."

"Should we blast?"

"If you do not . . . Captain Northern . . . then I fear . . . that I would be . . . obliged to borrow . . . your weapon . . . and do it . . . myself."

"In that case, might as well do this right. Laura, get your power gun out. I think these boltlike things here are hinges. We can blast these, and the door should come off."

Suddenly Laura was not so gung-ho. She realized that she was afraid. She wanted to simply turn around and run from there as fast as she could but she contained the urge. "My intuition is acting up, sir, and what it's telling me isn't good."

"Look, you fickle female," said Northern. "You were allowed to come along on the condition that you obeyed orders. Now get out that gun!"

Laura flashed him a glare, muttering under her breath. She definitely had a bad feeling about this, but her sworn loyalty to Captain Northern and her continued curiosity made her obey.

"Right. Now Shontill and Bey—stand out of the way. This door is going to be off in two shakes of a lamb's tail, and maybe we're actually going to get to the bottom of this blasted ultra-dimension business. Dr. Mish will be so pleased."

He's strangely excited, Laura thought, and not acting as cool as usual. What was it about this dimension that got everyone so hot and bothered, from her little brother to Dr. Mish? Northern was definitely not acting in an advisable fashion. Now it was his turn to be obsessive-compulsive.

She set her power gun to max and aimed at the hinge Northern had indicated.

"Now!" Northern said, louder than necessary.

Twin spurts of energy blasted into the bolts, easily blowing them off, leaving holes where they had been. The door rocked, then settled on supports, creating a partial opening.

"You think another blast is necessary, Shontill?" asked Northern.

"No," replied the alien.

They let the door cool for a moment, then Shontill easily ripped it off, allowing it to hang to one side like a flap of metallic skin.

The next room was partially obscured by a screen of sparkling haze. That the chamber was huge, cavernous, was easy to ascertain.

Then their eyes adjusted and Laura could make out that this was no mere repair dock. She couldn't help but gasp.

"Well, folks," said Captain Northern. "I do believe we've located something here."

Chapter Eight

The strident colors of the scene before them were particularly shocking after the black and white of the slanting corridors. For a long moment, motionless and silent save for the rasping of their breathing, transmitted through the radios, they could only stare at the sight before them.

The scene was like something from Dante's *Inferno* superimposed over his *Paradise*, filmed in Maxitech Depth Color. Only it wasn't a movie, it was real: a huge portal, simultaneously a pit and entrance, ridged with boiling, curling gases, studded with rainbow helixes on its sides like cilia in an esophagus. Debris was caught on the thorny helixes, the wire, steel, and glass of starships wavering languidly in an invisible current. The tunnel seemed to go on forever, sparkling and misty, crackling here and there with power surges. Something like stars glittered at the opposite end, alien yet somehow inviting. The whole thing seemed to throb with a corroscating energy, a patient slow maelstrom of mystery, awaiting victims.

"I have seen some weird things in my life," said Captain Northern, "but none tops this!"

"Stand away!" said Shontill. "I go . . . I go!" He made toward the entryway to the portal.

"Wait a moment, Shontill," said Northern, attempting to restrain him. "How do you know for sure this is what you're looking for? You're going to just dive on down there in your pressure suit? Let's check this out a moment."

Shontill stopped reluctantly, his large eyes gazing with almost human longing down into the abyss far deeper than the bottom of the starship.

Laura, meantime, still felt forboding stirring deep inside her, tugging her away from the edge of the precipice even as something exterior pulled her toward it. "Damn, Northern, all I gotta say is that I really don't like this!"

"Doesn't look real inviting does it?" the captain said. "What are you getting on your sensor board, Ratham?"

"So much data, it's still working on it, sir," said the lieutenant. "But so far we're reading the edges almost solidly plated with attilium. For proper analysis we're going to have to plug the recordings into our main computer when we get back."

"Let me take a look at that thing," Laura said, holding out her hands. "I've had sensor-board training and can read a lot of things before they start showing up."

Northern nodded to the lieutenant, who gave up the device. Laura glanced at the liquid quartz displays, the needles and dials. Almost immediately she detected the something amiss that her gut feeling had warned her about.

"Captain," she cried. "We've got to get out of here!"

"What are you talking about?" a baffled Northern asked, and like a bit of punctuation, the first tremor hit.

The force knocked them all off balance, tearing them from their magnetic moorings. A rough swirl of bright orange and red flashed through the portal like a stylized flame—and Laura could feel a force like strong gravity sucking them toward the doorway.

Ratham Bey, closest to the doorway, was yanked through. "Help!" he called, eyes alive with terror as the invisible force dragged him into the pit.

Shontill reached for him, but it was too late. Whatever force had caught the lieutenant was stronger out near the middle of the portal. It dragged him down, screaming, with surprising quickness, until Bey was reduced to speck size, then simply winked away, his scream lingering in everyone's ears.

"We've started some kind of chain reaction!" Laura managed to screech before the next tremor hit. Everything loose in the passageway fluttered as though struck by a gust of wind.

"I must go!" cried Shontill, surging toward the opening to follow Bey. But the door that they had blasted open suddenly

rocked back on its hinges, flapping shut. Its edge slammed
Shontill hard, his harsh grunt echoing through Laura's helmet
as he floated upward, unconscious.

"Grab him before that force starts sucking again!" cried
Northern. "I don't want to lose him."

Laura's impulse was to ignore the order, to simply turn and
rush back to the shuttle. All her danger signals, intuitive and
otherwise, were up full. This place was not stable, to say the
least! But instinct was reined in by her concern for Northern.
What the hell was going on inside of her? she wondered.

"He wanted to take a dive, Northern!" she said. "Let him!
We've got to get out of here and we don't have time to fool
with him! This place is going to blow!"

"You heard my order, dammit!" Northern growled angrily.
"You grab one side and I'll take the other!"

Laura opened her mouth to protest but realized there wasn't
time. She had to decide, and instantly she did, though the decision had nothing to do with instinct or intuition.

She took hold of one of Shontill's limply dangling forward
limbs, made sure of her magnetized footing, then started to
move. Sweat beaded her forehead and she could see from the
lights in Northern's helmet that he was perspiring as well, his
face ashen.

"Okay, Captain, but we've got to hurry or none of us is
going to make it outta here!"

For once, Laura was grateful for the previously awkward
weightlessness in the chamber. They'd never have been able to
haul this limp monster back in any kind of gravity. Even now
it was difficult to squeeze through the narrow portions of the
passageway and still be mindful of their hurry.

As soon as they passed the radio interference barrier,
Gemma Naquist's static-riddled voice erupted in their head-
phones. ". . . of there! Red alert! I'm reading threshold level
energy interaction, indicative of disruptive potential. Captain
Northern, dammit, do you read me? If you don't already
know it, this whole derelict is going to blow up. What did you
do?"

"Prepare airlock for unconsious alien, Midshipman,"
replied Northern. "Pull him in, and then Laura and I are next.
We lost Bey."

A moment of silence, then Naquist said, "Roger. Over."

By this time, the passageways were vibrating intensely, filled

with bits and pieces of the alien ship floating, detached, which
Laura and Northern had to make their way through. Rasping
breath sounded in Laura's ears. She wasn't sure if it was her
own or Northern's. Sweat stung her eyes as the temp-con-
troller of the suit struggled to compensate.

A shrill keening interrupted further radio transmissions;
Laura had to shut off communications to keep the noise from
splitting her eardrums. No matter. She knew what they had to
do.

It seemed a frustrating eternity, but finally the running
lights of the shuttle shone through the darkness of the passageway. Laura and Northern navigated Shontill into the open
airlock. Immediately, it closed.

"C'mon, c'mon, hurry!" Laura whispered tensely, and she
could read the same urgency in Northern's eyes.

A bit of debris clunked against Laura's helmet. A glance
behind her showed a barely visible stretch of hallway crum-
pling in upon itself. Even as she saw this, she noticed a tug of
force, as though that awful place, that horrible portal, were
tugging her back toward it.

Something to grab onto! She looked around, seeing nothing.

The door wasn't open yet! Was Gemma having trouble
hauling that goddamn alien through? She cursed the thing
even as she grappled for a hold in the alien wall. Something
was sticking out; she grabbed it. Northern was on the other
side, holding onto an abutment.

Dammit, Gemma! her mind screamed. *Hurry!*

The force grew stronger.

Finally, the airlock opened. There was a good four meters
between it and her.

Laura took out her gun, thumbed it to low, steady power,
and used it as a retrorocket. It was difficult, but she made it,
grabbing hold of a handle to keep her in place then reholster-
ing the power gun.

Northern followed her lead. By the time she grabbed him
and helped him in, it was more than evident that the whole
alien artifact was shaking apart.

The door cycled closed. Air rushed in. Before the process
was complete, however, Northern tried his radio and found
the jamming effect gone.

"Disengage and head back for the *Starbow*, full speed!" Northern ordered.

"Aye, aye, sir," Naquist's voice crackled over the radio. Almost immediately they were slammed against the side of the lock by the G-force from the thrust; Midshipman Naquist had been all ready for that particular command.

A green all-clear light flashed, and Northern pushed his way into the interior of the shuttle. Laura saw over his shoulder that Shontill, still unconscious, was haphazardly strapped into a grav-couch and Naquist was harnessed at the controls.

"What happened?" Naquist demanded immediately.

"Later," Northern said breathlessly. "Just radio ahead and ready the docking bay, then as soon as we've boarded get the goddamn shield up and get away from this thing."

"First Mate Thur is fully cognizant of the situation and is prepared to do just that, sir."

"Good, let's just hope that hellish thing gives us a chance to get back, if it's really going to go up."

"We must have tripped some bit of wire," Laura said, getting rid of her helmet, relishing the cool air of the shuttle's interior. "Dunno if it was a trap or if we just goofed. Goddamn alien almost got us all killed."

Northern explained briefly what they had found and also Rathem Bey's fate. Just as he finished, Shontill awoke, raging. With no difficulty, he broke the straps then tore his helmet off. His face was swathed in a dark ugly purple. He looked out of control.

"Go back!" he screeched. "We must . . . go back!" Then the alien broke out into incomprehensible clickings and clatterings: its alien tongue.

The captain's cool, though, had returned. Calmly, he lifted his gun and said in a clear, articulate voice, "Now, Shontill, my friend. Laura Shemzak and I just risked our lives to rescue you from certain death, but I have no compunction about blowing your head off if you act up anymore. You will stay put, and we will go back to the *Starbow* and put her into a place where it cannot be affected if your people's vessel blows up."

The sight of the gun seemed to calm Shontill immensely; at least he made no more threatening motions, gestures, or sounds.

"The way . . . will be . . . closed up," the alien said hopelessly.

"If that's the way it is, fella, that's the way it is," Laura said. "But we got a look at it, you've proved your point. No attilium in our bags, true, but we got a detailed set of recordings on the phenomenon, right here in this baby." She tapped the portable sensor board. "And once we find my brother and he puts his head together with Dr. Mish, ain't no way we're not going to be able to get through to this Omega Space, or whatever you call it."

Shontill slumped back motionless, his expression unreadable.

"Vu-plates don't look good, Captain," said Naquist.

Laura glanced at the full picture of the Frin'ral artifact floating like an angry metal thundercloud in the infinite sky. Traceries of lightninglike energy jagged around the ragged periphery like demon claws, ripping and tearing the hull to tatters. Debris orbited the ship closely, like hovering insects above a dead and rotting body.

Captain Northern turned to Naquist and she had an answer ready for him: "We're going as fast as we can and I've got my finger on the shield erection button."

Northern shook his head. "Those energies we saw . . . felt. Amazing. I don't want to be anywhere close to that aperture when it seals up."

"Two minutes to docking bay," said Naquist.

"I can't help but feel as though that portal was left like that . . . on purpose," said Northern. "As though the Frin'ral knew that there would be people wanting to find their secret . . . and they wanted to deal with them." He turned to Laura. "We should have listened to you, Laura. I'm sorry."

Laura was taken aback by his apology. She should have learned by now, she thought, not to be surprised by anything Captain Tars Northern did. He was nothing if not erratic.

"I don't know what it was, Captain. I can't analyse it and I can't say whether or not it's going to show up on the sensor readings . . . but it felt real bad."

"Noted. We'll pay more attention to your intuitions in the future. I think I'm already putting more faith in them than I do in Dansen Jitt's."

Seconds later the docking bay had swallowed them up and they'd locked into the shuttle's compartment.

Northern radioed the bridge immediately. "Get the hell out of here quick, Thur!"

"Impulse engines on full, sir, and shields up. What happened?"

"We'll tell you when we get up there." He looked over at the alien. "Shontill, perhaps you'd like to go to your cabin. Anything you need we'll be glad to supply."

"I wish . . . to observe . . . what occurs," said the alien. "I can promise . . . I will be . . . of no danger. I am resigned . . . to the ship's fate."

"Very well, then. Let's head up."

The crew were at their stations, efficiently making sure that the *Starbow* was heading out of harm's way. As the shuttle exploration team arrived on the bridge, still in their pressure suits, grimy and sweaty and upset, they were met with the sight of the central vu-tank swelling with the Frin'ral derelict from which they had barely escaped with their lives.

Captain Northern immediately assumed command with the ease of a man donning a suit tailored specifically to him.

"How long till safe entry of Underspace?" he asked Thur, who had stepped over by the sensor station.

"About five minutes, sir," the First Mate replied.

Dr. Mish, in his usual post by the sensors, looked up, quite agitated. "I think we are safe at this distance and with the shields—"

"And you want to hang around to record the portal sealing," Captain Northern finished for him, annoyed. "Dammit, fellow, it's your ass I'm watching out for here!"

Dr. Mish grinned. "And shouldn't I be the one to decide the state of the armor about that ass?"

"In this kind of situation, I wonder. You're entirely too obsessed with this goddamn Omega Space, Mish! I saw it, felt it, and it's immensely powerful."

"We've got detailed sensor recordings, Doctor," Laura offered, wanting to get far away from that place herself.

Mish shook his head. "Insufficient. Sensors show the reactions inside that ship, at the portal, are near critical. At the moment a slow implosion effect, somehow triggered by you, is pulling the entirety of the vessel inside the portal bit by bit. Hence the crackup more than obvious in the screen. Presumably without sufficient stasis devices, the rent in normal space will simply seal up. During that time, if we observe the spectrum fluctuations, record the energy emanations et al, we might learn a great deal not only about the portal, but about Omega Space itself."

"But Doctor, at the threat of our lives?"

"I assure you, dear boy, we shall be at the point where at the least sign of danger we can instantly sink into Underspace. Besides, I should warn you, because of the nature of these energies, I suspect we are no safer in the Underspace dimension than in more normal planes."

"Well then," Captain Northern said, his tension fading somewhat. "If that's the way it is—"

Dansen Jitt looked up from his plotting controls. "Course all set for resumption, sir, and might I add that if you'd like my opinion—"

"Thank you Mr. Jitt, but no thank you," replied the Captain. Since he had spoken to Dr. Mish, Laura noted that his spirits and aplomb seemed to climb back to their normal cocky level. It was almost as though he depended upon Mish, and the *Starbow*, for buttressing his personality. "We symbiotes shall honor our host's wishes," he said, saluting the doctor. "Presumably for the interests of all."

Laura was too tired to object; besides, she had no particular instinctive impulses one way or the other. However, she was only too glad to take Northern's suggestion of strapping herself into a grav-couch to prepare for any possible disturbances. The rest of the crew did so as well—except for Shontill, who would not fit but agreed to be tied to a strong railing support. His wide, moist eyes never left the vu-tank image of his race's derelict portal craft. What strange alien thoughts flitted through that brain of his? Laura wondered. What emotions . . . ? To have the hope of contacting one's lost brethren again after so many drifting, lonely years placed tantalizingly in reach, then snatched away. . . .

Still, the alien watched all the proceedings of the next few minutes stoically, green eyes unblinking, brown crest running calm and unruffled from squat skull to tail.

It did not take long for the promised implosion to reach its end. Laura and the crew members watched as the gigantic Frin'ral ship crumpled in upon itself, exuding a panoply of bright phantasmagoric energies like degenerating halos. When the ship was entirely gone, only a large oval distortion, a

wavery bit of somethingness against the starfield, was left
—and then that, too, winked out.

"Got that, Dr. Mish?" asked Captain Northern.

"Yes, though it's going to take a while to analyze," returned the white-haired extension of the starship.

"Good. Gentlepeople, please prepare for resumption of
Underspace course for Snar'shill, Dominus Cluster," said
Captain Northern, who then turned to Shontill. "Well, Shontill, good fellow, sorry it did not work out the way you wanted
. . . but you're still alive, and we've got some new and valuable
data."

"I regret . . . the loss . . . of your lieutenant," the alien
replied, unbuckling himself. "It should have been I who . . .
fell into . . . the portal."

"And gotten killed?" Laura said, bouncing out of her
chair. "Sorry about Bey and all that, but you've got to survive
to get what you want."

"There's no proof that Bey died, Laura," Northern replied,
scratching his nose solemnly. "And as far as I'm concerned,
this steps up considerably my commitment to getting the facts
on this Omega Space. Bey was a good crew member and I'd
like to take that statement out of past tense, if I possibly can."

"I don't understand, Northern," said Laura. "You weren't
so hot on going back for another crew member when I first
met you."

"You refer to Kat Mizel, I presume," said Northern, grinning. "An entirely different situation, I assure you. Now, in
the meantime, we have an opportunity to deal with your little
problem, Laura."

"You mean those implants," Laura murmured.

"Yes, and because of the delay it will not be necessary for
Mish to use his Genghis Khan model for the operation. You
can do it yourself, can't you, Mish?"

"Certainly."

"First thing in the morning, then, Laura, after you've gotten a bit of rest. We've not had an exactly uneventful day.
Besides, that way the doctor can prepare for the operation,
right, Doctor?"

"And it will be a great pleasure, my dear, to be of service."

Laura looked around at the assembled bridge crew. She
couldn't get over the amount of interest and caring reflected in
their eyes. It was difficult to accept that the people around you

cared a jot; she certainly wasn't used to it after working for years for as cold an employer as the Federation and dealing with the vile, ambitious people the system produced to maintain the starways. She even caught a flash of sympathy, if not empathy, in Silver Zenyo's usually catty eyes.

The emotion this aroused was difficult to deal with. Laura laughed it off. "Well, this won't be the first time someone's been mucking around in my interior."

Before now, it didn't seem she had the equipment to feel anything about getting all manner of stuff planted inside of her. Now, though, it felt . . . funny.

She patted Shontill on a shoulder. "Sorry about all this. I think I know how you feel."

Shontill looked at her with what could have been interpreted as a bemused expression.

"You want somebody to walk you back to your place?" Laura asked. "I'm headed to my own cabin, and it's right on the way, I think."

Shontill looked over to Captain Northern, who simply nodded and said, "Go ahead, Shontill. You've got to realize that you really aren't alone, you great beast. You're with us, aren't you?"

Laura imagined that it must have made a very odd picture, her diminutive self leading away a seven-foot alien. Even as they walked, Laura felt bad that she had wanted to leave him behind, unconscious.

What was happening to her? she wondered. Where once she had been tight and linear, now she was getting kind of unstuck and loose.

The thought of the unconscious alien made her say, "Oh, Shontill, we never checked to see about wounds."

"I thank you . . . for your practicality . . . Laura Shemzak," returned the alien. "But I am . . . as you may recall . . . highly metamorphic and regenerative."

"I wish," said Laura, "that was true with me."

She also wished she could deal with some aspects of her life she could never divulge, not even to these people who had become her friends.

Chapter Nine

All her life she'd been surrounded by machines. At first the idea of actually being riddled with them was not at all threatening. After all, cyborg implantations were quite normal on Earth and its associated planets. There were thousands of doctors specializing in that kind of adaptive interface surgery.

But Laura had never before been actually operated on by a machine behind the machines. She had mentioned this to Dr. Mish and he had simply pooh-poohed the notion. He was as well equipped as anyone to do the job, he pointed out, and if something went wrong . . . Well, he had plenty of ocular circuits to replace her eyes with!

For some reason that didn't comfort Laura much. Even though she had a lot of high-tech paraphernalia buried in her, for all intents and purposes she was quite human, and she meant to keep it that way.

For Dr. Mish the difference between flesh and metaplast was miniscule; he found dealing surgically with Laura a fairly simple task once he studied his X-rays and had scanned her anatomy. Her bioengineering doctors had sewn her back up in such a way that servicing her devices was child's play. Indeed, Laura had accessibility to many of them herself—and her blip-ship was equipped and programmed to perform the occasional fine tuning necessary. Her skull implants, however, needed outside expert service, even though they had the equivalent of a sealed doorway, easily unlatched by the proper surgical procedure.

Laura chose to remain conscious during the proceedings. Her head had to be shaved and she regretted this silently because Tars Northern had not found her appealing in short hair. It was a factor she instantly dismissed, railing at herself for thinking such silly thoughts.

About an hour into the operation, Laura almost regretted that she asked to remain awake. Sleep would have relieved the boredom. Dr. Mish was too involved with his work to provide small talk, and it was truly a drag to simply sit there in a sterile field with your head hanging open. Still, she wanted to remain awake. She certainly didn't want Dr. Mish to go exploring in places she preferred to keep secret. He hadn't noticed the drug dispenser the first time because he hadn't been looking for it. Though it was placed far away from her head, she didn't want him to find it now.

"Now, Laura," Dr. Mish said, "you may lose your sight for just a few moments, but there's no way around that. It's quite a tiny device, but there are all kinds of wires leading hither and thither and I may cut a few of the wrong ones."

"Swell," said Laura. She felt like a lab rat who knew too much. On the wall were all manner of readout screens and blinking lights. Nearby was a replica of her head: a holograph rendering her flesh-and-bone parts transparent, so as to show the intricate array of the cyborg mechanisms. "I don't suppose you have any music you can play," she said. "This is getting dull."

"Oh, you should have said something earlier," replied the doctor. Light contemporary classical music filtered from speakers somewhere, like tinkling gushes of waterfalls.

"You haven't got any clangor, huh?" said Laura, slightly disappointed.

"Clangor?" Dr. Mish stood back, blinking his eyes, cyborg surgery tools before him like praying mantis legs.

"New music, guy! I fill up on the stuff every time I can, though I haven't explored the XT-9's tape banks yet."

"No. I do have some ancient roll and rock which might please your ears."

"No. This stuff sounds about the same to me," she said, settling back and trying to relax.

"Laura," said Dr. Mish. "This small tiny box here, have

you got any idea of its purpose?''

Laura shifted her eyes to the holograph. Dr. Mish had outlined the tiny thing in a red light.

"Extra memory storage? I got them tucked away all over. Micro microchip. Talk about angels on the head of a pin!''

"Ah yes," he said, studying its signals closer. "I should have realized. Mind if I check it for content? This could store additional elements of the program that interfered with your natural motor functions and made you shoot at the image of your brother.''

"You can do that?'' Laura said skeptically.

"Oh yes, I can tap these bytes and make a copy in my own storage area, then put it up on a screen. If it's the kind of program I think it is, then we can erase it. If it's something else that's harmless, we can just leave it be.''

Laura found it impossible to shrug, but she tried. "Sure. Go ahead.''

Dr. Mish brought down a hanging bit of apparatus, slipped it into her head, and connected it to the item in question. A touch of a button, a hum of energy, and the screen began to jiggle and dance with numbers and figures.

"My goodness," said Dr. Mish, taken aback. "Quite a slew of stuff!''

"Told you about the memory storage," she said as database items occasionally froze on the screen, giving her an opportunity to scrutinize some of the material. "Wait a moment. That's strange-looking stuff. Let's get a closer look at it, Mish!''

"First things first, Laura," said Dr. Mish. "Let's get this implant off.''

Mish bent over, lights reflecting bizarrely from his machines, and worked for some moments. Laura felt a pressure on the back of her left eye, then it was gone.

"I can still see!'' she announced, a little bit relieved.

"A very simple job, actually. They must have put this in hurriedly.''

"Yes they did, as a matter of fact.''

"Funny, it seems to be complete, with its own micro-CPU tapping into your energy nodes . . . and its own programming," said Dr. Mish, after a detailed analysis scan of the device. "A program in your auxiliary memory would be redundant, and perhaps even intrusive. Let me get you back together here and we'll see what we've tapped out of it. I'm surprised you don't have personal access."

"Maybe with the blip, Doctor, but frankly there's stuff in me that even I don't know how it works!"

"Hmm," said Dr. Mish. "Could be involved with piloting your ship, you think?" His thin and delicate hands made quick work of placing things back in order inside her skull.

"Haven't the faintest, but I'm damned curious!" Laura returned impatiently.

As quickly as he could, Dr. Mish resealed her bald head. "Now we can either slap on some growth encouragement or get you some kind of wig."

"Wig's out," Laura said. "Try that other stuff . . . seems to do wonders for the captain's beard."

During the operation she had attempted to pump the doctor for information on Tars Northern, to no avail. Mish pleaded the necessity for concentration and had thus avoided telling anything he knew.

There was no mistaking it—Dr. Mish had to know it all. There was definitely some kind of bond between the two of them that could not be penetrated by mere outsider inquiries.

But then that was part of the game, Laura thought: find out just what was really going on in this odd starship filled with efficient pi-mercs who claimed to be rebels but had no army to back them up. A motley bunch of galactic warriors!

Still, she knew there were ways to find things out other than asking.

After getting a sprinkle and rub of the hair-growth encourager, Laura turned her attention to the strange data that had been stored inside her.

"I'm working up translations," said Dr. Mish. "It seems to be in a number of languages and codes, but nothing impenetrable. Hmm, let's see."

He diddled with controls, glancing up occasionally at the screen.

"I don't remember being fed any of this," Laura said, bemused. "Doesn't look like blip-ship stuff. Looks like raw data from some kind of coordinating computer to me."

Dr. Mish seemed a little more aware of just what this material seemed to be. A very human look of total astonishment crossed his face.

"Oh, my," he said, blinking at a section of readout. "Oh,

dear me." He turned to Laura. "Where did you get this?" he demanded, no longer the mild-spoken scientist but a very agitated and excited person. "This . . . this could change everything!"

Laura looked at the indecipherable stuff then turned back to Mish. "Huh?" she said.

Chapter Ten

"At least I'm not bored," said Cal Shemzak to his manservant.

"Sir?"

"I said, Wilkins, that I have to be grateful to the Jaxdron that they are keeping me entertained."

Absently, he lifted a knight above the chess board. A hiss of static sounded in the earpiece of his headset, as though the monotone that barked response moves were eager with anticipation.

Lazily, Cal put the knight back in its position in front of his queen's bishop and smiled to himself, hoping his procrastination annoyed whatever Jaxdron machine was assigned to him.

Or perhaps it was a Jaxdron in the flesh—or chitin, or whatever they wore—amusing itself.

"Yes, sir. I've placed clean clothing in your room," the tall slender-nosed man said in a clipped accent. "And I've taken the liberty of pressing your suit for the meeting later this week."

"Meeting?" said Cal. "What meeting?"

They sat in what Cal now called the Dream Room. This was where the Jaxdron made him dance to their illusions, which Cal had gotten used to and in fact rather enjoyed now, seeing them as a challenge. He'd been in several of them after the desert and robot scenario. Wars. Jungle chases. Space shootouts. All involved survival . . . and puzzles.

Now the Dream Room featured a pleasant beach. Hidden speakers provided the tranquil sound of rolling breakers to accompany the sparkling sand, the cheery sky, the lazy warmth.

Cal sat in a beach chair beside a table equipped with the chessboard. He wasn't forced to play chess but he found it like doodling with his mind and enjoyed it.

"Yes, sir. Did you not read the formal invitation?"

"I wasn't aware that I had mail call here, Wilkins." Cal sat up and gazed around him. "Hell, I'm not even sure where 'here' is."

His wanderings were, after all, limited to a corridor and a small sequence of rooms. He had not even been allowed to view the surface of the planet . . . if he was on a planet. For all he knew, he was on some mammoth starship still in transit.

"Yes, sir," replied Wilkins. "I left it on your desk this morning."

Cal ripped his headset off, throwing it across the chessboard, scattering pieces. "Hubba hubba, fella!" he cried, jumping up and running for the door. "This sounds interesting!"

He tore down the hallway and into the small cubicle which was his room in this comfortable prison. Sure enough, there on his dresser was a gilt-edged envelope embossed with a seal. He turned it over. It was addressed to Mr. Calspar Shemzak in expert calligraphy.

Eagerly, he ripped the envelope and tore out the enclosed invitation.

It read:

YOUR PRESENCE IS REQUESTED IN ROOM 27 FOUR DAYS
HENCE AT 12 NOON BY YOUR HOSTS FOR A PERSONAL
AUDIENCE CONCERNING YOUR ACTIVITIES HERE.

Room 27? Where the hell was that? Wilkins would know.

Maybe he was going to get a new room added to his little prison world. Perhaps even a room with a window, so that he could get some idea of where he was.

Cal sat down on his bed and sighed. A man with a less sound psychological makeup would never have stayed sane this long. Fortunately, Cal knew who he was. Cal knew to follow the *wo wei*, to go with the flow, to accept the reality that was the next moment, to approach it with no prejudice. . . .

Even as he lay on the bed relaxing, feeling the exciting promise of knowledge, he experienced another attack.

As usual, it began as a fading away of immediate sensation, like the gentle moments of disassociative logic before falling asleep. Then came the buzzing, the hum of some sort of contact. But with whom? He was much too involved with the experience to analyze.

. . . whisper . . . whisper . . .

. . . glimmer . . . glow . . .

A tumble of images, like a rainfall of pictures, soundless swirling in the wind . . .

He felt snippets of calculation, bits of formulas computated, solving of problems, as though he were some capacitor in a computer observing logic flow. And again, as always, he flashed on that image with the mirrors, then it was gone.

He knew he was in a room somewhere and the room was dark, knew there were others in the room . . .

. . . and by the emerging glow of candlelight, he could see that the others were . . .

. . . himself.

And they talked to him.

But their voices were soft and low, and he could not quite make out what they were saying, although he heard snatches of words and phrases which seemed to deal with some scientific problem. He felt hot, sweating, and he could hear the pound of his heart in his ear, growing unbearably loud.

His own faces approached him and they said, What is the Answer, Father? We live for the Answer, and only you are the—

Someone was shaking his arm.

"Sir? Sir, are you all right?"

His eyelids opened away from the land of reflection and refraction and he saw Wilkins staring down at him with a worried expression.

"The . . . reverie . . . again," Cal muttered. He'd had these things before, and each time they were more intense.

He sat up and Wilkins poured him a glass of water.

"They're not like the tests, Wilkins," Cal said, water dribbling down his chin. "They're not puzzles, dammit, they don't make any sense!'' He grabbed the manservant's lapels. ''Why do your masters do this, fellow? Why?''

''I shall report the matter immediately, sir,'' Wilkins said, gently removing his charge's fingers. ''Now, can I get you a pill?''

''No,'' Cal replied, recovering his aplomb. He kept forgetting to withhold his thoughts and emotions from this character. Wilkins, whoever or whatever he was, worked for the enemy, not him. ''No, I'm fine. I think it must just be a side effect of all this testing, Wilkins. I'm fine. You needn't report anything.''

''Very good, sir.'' The manservant's eyes flicked about the room, caught the sight of the torn-apart envelope and letter. ''Ah. I see you found your invitation.''

''Yes. But Wilkins, where the hell is room 27? Am I going to get expanded access to other rooms in this place?''

''I should think so, sir,'' Wilkins replied coolly and non-committally. ''I have taken the liberty of reassembling your chess game. Would you care to return to a beach scene or shall I adjust the climate to something else?''

Cal Shemzak opened his mouth, and if he had let out what was on his tongue, he would have released a torrent of pent-up anger and frustration. But he held his tongue and bided his time.

He could wait a few more days until he actually confronted the Jaxdron, and they could respond directly.

''No, Wilkins, the beach scene was quite restful. Let me take a shower and I'll be right out. Oh, and could I have some sandwiches, please?''

''Very good, sir.''

A suspicion had dawned upon Cal Shemzak . . . a suspicion that would explain a great deal.

Chapter Eleven

The two identical cyborgs sat in their cabin playing chess.

Though they looked exactly like Cal Shemzak, they were not. In fact, interviews and tests and scans of their systems revealed that though they each owned small fragments of Cal Shemzak, at least in personality and memory, neither were complete replicas in any way.

To be sure, the crew of the *Starbow* had thoroughly checked them for any possibility of threat to the ship or the crew and found the pair extremely weak physically, with no sign of weapons or malicious intent. Their general docility reflected Cal's accepting nature, at least on the surface. Yet there was more to these constructs than met the eye, be it human or electronic.

Cal One, as he was called, dressed mostly in blue for identification purposes, captured one of his opponent's knights. Cal Two, in red, countered with a move of his bishop which placed the other player's queen in jeopardy.

At the top of the room, to either side, spy eyes tracked their every movement and electronic bugs in the wall recorded every spoken interchange. Thus far the twins had simply played games—not merely chess, but backgammon, scrabble, bochoi —all board games. For security reasons a computer terminal could not be given to them—though the "Shemzak twins" seemed harmless and were certainly nothing less than totally cooperative; to place access into the *Starbow's* computers might tempt fate. So, actual physical facsimiles of the games, usually played via computer, were constructed in Dr. Mish's shop and given to the pair to while away the time they were not being interrogated or analyzed.

As Cal One's hand reached out for the next move to protect his queen, his forefinger gently brushed his twin's knuckles. In this briefest of physical contacts an entire dialogue was exchanged:

»Brother, the time approaches«

»Yes, I sense the Communication imminent«

»We must prepare ourselves for the Roles«

»Aye, our Great Playing shall be glorious«

»Our Masters have selected their Targets cleverly«

»Much glory shall be derived from the interchange of Points«

»But will Victory belong to the Jaxdron«

»That, brother, is the Continued Mystery that underlines and defines all experience«

»We can only wait for the Calling«

»The Calling shall surely come soon«

»Praise the Mighty and Manipulative Jaxdron, and let their Conquering Might hang long on the mandibles of their Eternal Ancestors«

»In the meantime, brother, I shall soundly thrash you in these simple games«

»The Challenge is heard, brother, and I shall renew the onslaught. The very air is bloody with our conflict, and the cries of death and vexation are foreshadows to the reality to occur upon this vessel, when the Partnership occurs«

»Hail to the Jaxdron, and watch me chew up these pieces in my fangs of intellect«

. . . and the hand broke contact, and fell upon a pawn, which it moved forward one space.

Captain Tars Northern tossed back his last bit of brandy and looked up from the sheath of print-outs.

He grinned, but his eyes still showed the astonishment that had appeared in them when Dr. Mish and Laura Shemzak had walked in with the news. "It certainly is something, all right." He looked at Laura. "Where the hell did you get this stuff, anyway, girl? And what else might be hiding away in some hidden memory cells in that slender little figure of yours?"

Laura fidgeted uncomfortably in her chair. "Only this, Northern. And the reason is simple. They forgot to debrief me."

"Sounds racy, Laura," said Northern, leafing back through the thick pile of papers. "Dr. Mish, let me get this straight. Just by happenstance, you came upon information tucked away in Pilot Shemzak's auxiliary memory nodes which reveals that the Jaxdron have infiltrated at least one of the Federation's outposts without formally conquering it?"

"The information would seem to indicate that, Captain." Mish took the brandy container from the table and placed it back in the cabinet.

Captain Northern hardly seemed to notice, looking down again at the translation. "A lot of this is just gibberish to me."

"And to us as well," said Mish. "But from the hints and clues scattered through the text, your conclusion is exactly the same as ours."

"From the beginning, Laura," said Northern after she took a deep breath and shook her long hair. "How did you get this material?"

"It's fairly simple, Captain," Laura said, getting up and pacing. "From time to time, as an employee of the Federation, I received assignments as an undercover Intelligence agent. Just before I learned of my brother's capture by the Jaxdron, it just so happened that I had infiltrated Pax Industries on Walthor."

"Yes, yes, Laura," Northern said, tapping the paper pile brusquely. "Pax Industries. Walthor. Prominent names here. But why should the Federation ask an agent to infiltrate its own world, its own company?"

"Easy. To check its security measures. I was assigned to get to the core of their main computer and tap Top Secret databases. I did so surprisingly easily. I reported to the company's president, who had no idea of what I was up to. I told him I'd send him a report, which I did, during the trip back to Earth. However, in tapping the database, I also stored a good deal of it in available space. I guess in the hoopla concerning my brother, they accepted my report and forgot to actually take a look at what I'd tapped. Hell, Captain, I'm as surprised as anyone! I'd forgotten all about that info and I certainly didn't think it had anything to do with the Jaxdron!"

Northern shook his head. "Strange stuff. I trust, Dr. Mish,

that you're working more on this material. Apparently the Jaxdron are manufacturing the equivalent of hyper-radio bugs within the various highly advanced technological products produced on Walthor, and then shipped throughout the Federation. Electronic spies over the width and breadth of Federation space, collecting information and God knows what else. Laura, did you see anything suspicious on Walthor? Any indication of Jaxdron activity?''

"I wouldn't know what a Jaxdron looked like if it came up and bit me, Northern! It was an alien world. There are always strange things on an alien world. I had a job and I did it quickly and well. I can't tell you anymore right now."

"You do know the planet well enough, though."

"Certainly."

Northern considered for a moment, then slapped the table with finality. "Excellent. Then we've got a brief detour to take, my friends."

"What?" Laura said. "You're saying we're going to go to Walthor? But Cal isn't there! Cal has been taken to Snar'shill!" She stood up from her chair, fuming.

"Yes, and we have that information courtesy of the Jaxdron, almost as though they dare us to chase after them," Captain Northern said, eyes turning chilly black. "Well, if there's more than we can do except chase after them, whistling in the dark, then I certainly intend to do it. We are equipped with very little information on this race. If we can get more from Pax Industries, then that's what we're going to do!"

"Goddammit!" Laura cried, stalking about, livid. "This doesn't feel good to me."

"It seems utterly rational to me, Laura," interjected Dr. Mish.

"But you promised! We've got to get Cal—before the Jaxdron do something awful to him!"

"Your emotions are quite understandable," Northern said, standing up and attempting to calm her. He put a hand to her shoulder and it was shrugged off. "But we have to look at this calmly, and as Dr. Mish reminds us, rationally. We are a single starship up against an inscrutable alien race and a malignant group of fellow human beings to boot. We need every bit of the puzzle to succeed here. If we can find some more pieces on Walthor, then that's where we have to go. And we desperately need your cooperation. So be a good girl, won't you, and play along."

"I don't have any choice, do I?" Laura said, eyes blazing.

"No, you don't, but take heart knowing that this material," he patted the paper, "could well mean not only the recovery of your brother, but the hope for humanity against the Jaxdron threat to our space."

"I'm so goddamn thrilled," she said, turning to Dr. Mish. "Well, now that that's settled, do I have a clean enough bill of health to have a session with those Cal clones? I guess I could use a couple of surrogate brothers right now."

"Of course, Laura," replied Dr. Mish. "You might actually learn more from them than we're able to."

Laura Shemzak nodded. "Right, and I'll bring them love from you guys too."

She left in a huff.

"A vibrant but unpredictable being," Dr. Mish commented.

"Yes," said Northern, going to the liquor cabinet.

Mish looked on with strong disapproval. "You've had enough for today, Tars. I haven't got my sensor board, but I can tell."

Northern shrugged, and grinned like a little boy after getting his hand caught in a cookie jar. "Save it for when I need it, eh, Mish?"

"I wish we didn't need it at all, my boy, but we can't fool with something so delicate, something that works. Perhaps later . . ."

"Good enough for me," Northern said, settling for cold soda water. He flipped a star-map projection on by his desk. "Now then, as long as we're going to be going that way now, I thought we'd make another previously unplanned stop."

"Oh?"

"Yes. We need . . ." Northern glanced over at the liquor cabinet. ". . . supplies, and I've a friend whose stores are plentiful." Northern grinned. "There are other reasons beyond that, of course."

Mish examined the spot where Northern's hand pointed. "Ah yes, that would be a fortuitous stop-off point."

Northern nodded. "Yes, Freeman Jonst is one of our few true friends, and Kendrick's Vision has always welcomed us."

Chapter Twelve

"Barbarians!" Overfriend Arnal Zarpfrin toured the destroyed buildings in the capital city of Kendrick's Vision. President Freeman Jonst walked uneasily by his side. "An outrage! They must be stopped. They must be pushed back to the forsaken holes they crawled from!"

"Please, Zarpfrin, if you could be more quiet!" said President Jonst, darting glances at the people milling around the crumbled masonry and metal, all that remained of the buildings touched by Jaxdron fire. "My people are not aware of your presence. They are still shocked and stunned by this assault on our home. It would not be wise to let them know at this point of your presence here on Kendrick's Vision. We have not even determined if there are any arrangements that can be made between our world and the Federated Empire."

"Just Federation will do," Zarpfrin said, smiling. "New image, don't you know." A neat man, he was overweight in a comfortable fashion, as though he had chosen it. Though he had come to Kendrick's Vision in his Federation military finest, for purposes of inconspicuousness during this tour, President Jonst had dressed him in mufti. He now wore an outfit indistinguishable from those worn by the members of the Forum. Zarpfrin took out a flannel handkerchief and delicately patted away the perspiration that had formed on his temples. "Yes, my friend, the Free Worlds and the Federation certainly have a multitude of differences. But we must stick together in strenuous times like these.''

''Now that you've viewed the damage, Overfriend,'' said Freeman Jonst, eyes flicking nervously over the devastation, nostrils still cringing at the awful stench of destruction, ''can we head back to our capitol building? We have much to iron out in negotiation.''

''All for the good of humanity, I am sure,'' said Zarpfrin, a solemn but also somehow pleased expression settling on his face. ''For the rock bottom principle of the Federation is survival of the human race, whatever shape or color or quality it finds itself in, on whatever planet.''

Freeman Jonst nodded his head soberly and escorted the Overfriend back to the car that had taken them there.

Jonst just wanted to make the deal and get this guy off his planet, pronto, before he stank the place up too badly.

Chapter Thirteen

When Laura entered their cabin, the cyborg copies of her brother Cal flinched.

"Don't worry fellows, I'm fixed," said Laura, slumping down onto a couch. Goddamn Tars Northern anyway! She had been looking forward to this and now the guy had ruined it by this stupid course change. She was so annoyed at him, she couldn't get much out of speaking with these things. She had so hoped that seeing them would relieve her yearning for her brother. But now she was so upset, that having them before her simply confused her.

"Hi, Laura," said Cal One, grinning with relief. "Good to see you. My memories are quite incomplete but I only remember good things about you. Except, of course, that business on Baleful, and Captain Northern explained that to us."

"Yes, Laura," said Cal Two. "I love you, you know, and I always will. I remember that promise and it hasn't changed."

Laura sat up. "I'm not sure this was wise," she said, looking from one to the other of the twins. "I'm getting these strange feelings . . . as though I really were with Cal, and yet that lie is just real obvious, plain as the nose on my face."

"Do you think that we're not confused, Laura?" said Cal One. "After all, we are beings ourselves and we're both stocked with your brother's memories. We feel toward you as your brother felt, we respond to you in ways your brother would—"

"And we do love you," put in the other. "I, for one, am awfully happy to see you. They won't let us do much except play games here. Do you remember the games we played, Laura? My first memory is of you when we were very young. And they are warm memories . . . warm memories in this cold universe."

"Yeah. I have lots of memories, guys," Laura said, relaxing a bit, getting past her initial difficulties, warming to this pair. They certainly seemed friendly enough. "But neither of you is really Cal, and that's damn hard to deal with."

"But Laura, in real ways we are your brothers," said one, beaming. "We understand you! We know why you want to save the real Cal Shemzak. . . . No one else truly can, can they?"

"And you will stay, won't you?" chimed in the other.

"Well, that's what I want to do," said Laura. "I guess I can work some things out with you . . . about Cal and me."

"Work things out?" said Cal Two. "What do you mean by that?"

"Guilt feelings, I suppose."

"Guilt feelings? About what? You've got nothing to feel guilty about!"

"For letting you go— I don't know, for a lot of things, I guess. Mainly for letting the system break us up. Maybe that's why I can't let you go . . . I mean, let Cal go. Why didn't we just run away? Instead, I let them do this to me." She gestured toward her body. "Let them turn me into something rough and ready, something sometimes I'm not sure I really want to be!"

"But we talked about it, Laura!" said Cal Two. "I can remember that we agreed it was the only hope we had. We bucked the system as long as we could in our own way. You know how I tried to crash the computers to change our life vectors. I went as far as I could, short of getting the contents of our brains rearranged! There was nothing else we could do but promise to see each other from time to time, as often as we could manage."

"The ways of the Federation are not mild," said Cal One. "We were lucky to have been able to make the space in which our relationship could grow, without the intrusion of authority."

"Well, I've told that authority where to stuff their oppression!" Laura said defiantly. "I've thrown my lot in with this bunch of rebels and I'm damned glad I have! They may be a bunch of loons but they seem to care about one another, and maybe that's what I need right now."

"I'm glad for you," said Cal One. "You always were one who needed a cause to believe in, Laura. First it was me, and now you have the *Starbow*."

"Cal Shemzak is still my first priority, and the crew here knows that."

"That's nice to know, Laura. I hope you remember us."

"You. You're just copies! And dammit, I'm so confused, sitting here, yakking with Cal clones, that I forgot why I came to talk to you. Why the hell were you made, anyway? I mean, why would the Jaxdron make copies of my brother?"

Cal One picked up a pawn and toyed with it. "As you might have deduced, we are certainly not complete models of your brother. Oh, we may look like him exactly, but inside . . . well, just from a short talk with us, you can already no doubt tell the difference."

"The captain gave me the report on your memories of your —I mean, my brother's—capture, his experiences aboard the Jaxdron ship . . . it's all very strange. . . . Tests, mazes, games . . ."

"Analyses, perhaps."

"They wanted him because of something he knew about Omega Space. That's why the Jaxdron kidnapped him and destroyed the project on Mulliphen. Maybe Cal was getting close to the secret, a secret the Jaxdron wanted. But how could they get that secret out of him by making cyborg clones like you?"

"We certainly would like to know that answer as well, Laura," said Cal Two. "We have been rather introspective about the reasons for our existence, though the first memories we have of any awareness of there being more than one Cal Shemzak was on Baleful."

"Yes, what happened on Baleful?" Laura wanted to know.

"We came into being in a rather pleasant atmosphere of hospitality, in that dome. None of us met the original Cal Shemzak. We were only in existence for perhaps two days before you arrived. We would have all greeted you, but Cally —we all have variations on your brother's names for purposes of differentiation—saw you first and ran to greet you and—"

"And then I shot him." Laura shivered. "Damn Zarpfrin's

eyes. He didn't want the Jaxdron to have my brother's knowledge and he figured I didn't have much of a chance of getting him out. Much better to rig me to shoot him automatically on sight."

Her voice was bitter. She looked away from the two of them; she felt as though she were in some sort of schismatic nightmare, communicating with two Cal Shemzaks. Everything she had battled for in the past few weeks seemed to be coming unglued—she had difficulty even with her sense of reality. The comfort she felt being near what looked and sounded like her brother was frustrated by the fact that this comfort was merely an illusion. She fought to hold back her tears.

"Dammit!" she said, feeling the weight of unchecked emotion strain at the thin dam of her composure. "I had so many questions I wanted to ask you, whoever you really are. And I can't. . . ." She turned away. "You both make me miss my real brother so much."

"But don't you realize that we understand this, Laura?" said Cal Two, going to her and placing his arm over her shoulder in a way entirely reminiscent of Cal. "Those of your crew can't possibly understand this, but we can. That's why, even though most assuredly we are not truly your brothers—perhaps not even totally human in a conventional sense—we still are honored with an extreme caring for you, and we want you to feel comfortable with us."

"This is much harder than I thought it would be," said Laura. "I think maybe we should continue this interview later."

"Whatever you say, our sister," said Cal Two, releasing his hold. "We have been secluded here and here we shall remain."

"Come and speak with us whenever you please," said Cal One.

Laura rushed from the room, sealing it behind her, unable to deal with the powerful emotions that flowed inside her.

Go to my cabin, she thought. Rest. Calm down. Compose myself.

But she knew she would come back. She needed these two, that was clear, even though they weren't her true brothers. She needed them just as she needed . . . other things. Things that got her through. . . .

She relocked the door from outside, as she had been instructed, then walked away, knowing she would return.

When Laura left their prison, their hands brushed again.
»The preliminaries went well, brother«
»Soon, the Masters shall broadcast«
»I feel the Changlings move amongst my very atoms«
»What confusion we shall cause«
»What havoc shall reign«
»Honor and glory to the True Victory«
»The Victory of the Jaxdron«
»Your move, brother, for my own victory is nigh«
»Spawn of a junk heap, you shall eat your words«
Grinning, the two set about to move their pieces again.

Chapter Fourteen

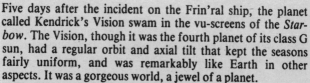

Five days after the incident on the Frin'ral ship, the planet called Kendrick's Vision swam in the vu-screens of the *Starbow*. The Vision, though it was the fourth planet of its class G sun, had a regular orbit and axial tilt that kept the seasons fairly uniform, and was remarkably like Earth in other aspects. It was a gorgeous world, a jewel of a planet.

The Vision was a place that knew the *Starbow* and its crew; knew and welcomed them. Freeman Jonst had tilted many a brew with Captain Tars Northern and kept him supplied from the mammoth stock of rare liquors from many planets, in return for news of Federation activity, Free World intercommunication, and the odd bit of contraband.

So the crew felt safe here, feeding the planet's guard satellites their usual code then settling into a wide, leisurely orbit of this pleasant planet of browns and blues, whites and greens smeared across the globe like paint on a palette.

The Underspace trip had been uneventful, the crew going about its usual business only slightly more anxious than usual, due to the nature of their quest. Still, in the lives they had accepted, the unexpected was a part of day-to-day events, and this extra bit of excitement was welcomed by all. Except Dansen Jitt, whose moroseness and prophesies of doom had increased to the point that Northern was no longer amused by them; he ordered Jitt to speak only when spoken to, or if he had something of an astrogational nature to say.

Laura made daily visits to speak to the copies of her brother Cal. She confided to Northern that she could only take so much of them—knowing they were not truly her brothers and their memories not the result of experience—but that she obtained a curious kind of satisfaction in being with them. Sometimes, these cyborg clones claimed sensations of contact with their progenitor; but Laura wasn't sure whether to believe them. The sensations carried no images with them, nor anything at all concrete. They were mere unsubstantiated claims. Their room had already been wired to pick up any indication of radio waves emanating or entering, and nothing was picked up. Apparently, this phenomenon was localized to the individual cyborgs. No alarm was taken.

Laura had also taken the opportunity to mingle with the crew, getting to know each of the members more individually, as much as her awkward social abilities would allow.

The term "motley crew" seemed custom-made for this bunch. Its thirty-odd components were quite odd indeed. There were individuals from all sections of the human-settled galaxy, all with radically different philosophies and viewpoints, yet all united in this common cause of rebellion against the insidious cultural enslavement exercised by the Federation over its planets and the Federation's implicit military threat to the autonomy of separated Free Worlds.

Originally, Laura learned, the distances and time between planets had allowed those farther away to rebel easily and sever ties with the Human Federated Empire. However, in the past hundred years, improvements on the hyperjump drives that carried vessels through the mathematical improbabilities of Underspace had improved remarkably. Where once the voyage had taken months and even years, the most distant colonies were now only weeks away from Earth. The Federation's weaponry and technology had increased also, while the non-united and often hermitlike independent worlds lagged behind, their fleets and defense systems comparatively primitive next to the Federation's newer weaponry.

This was the common dream, in one version or another, of all the crew members: to establish some kind of loose alliance between all the Free Worlds as a defense against the Federation. In the meantime they intended to aid the *Starbow*, preying on Federation shipping, as best they could with their particular specialties. The Free Worlds also relied on the

Starbow's analysis of new Federation technology. Once allied, the Free Worlds could build starships of equal power and ability, thus protecting their planets from both Jaxdron and the Federation.

This seemed a worthy goal to Laura. She certainly had lost all love and loyalty to the Federation, with its glib and smarmy Friends promising opportunity and security yet secretly controlling practically everything for the Greater Good of the State. Even the sort of rebellion Cal indulged in was merely slack in the leash, something in human nature that was expected and accommodated by the Federation lords of psychology, ultimately to be subtly crushed.

Aboard the *Starbow* Laura had the opportunity to think and talk about a great deal, and all the crew had remarked to one another about her sincere interest in overcoming her former doubt and cynicism. As for her abrasiveness and general bad manners, the crew members noticed she seemed more relaxed and friendly, in a coarse kind of way; less confrontational, certainly. Her sparring matches with Captain Northern continued but they became much more playful and affectionate. It was clear to everyone that each of them enjoyed getting one-up on the other, be the jokes verbal or practical.

However, despite her requests there were still parts of the *Starbow* that remained off limits to her. This sense of mystery would have troubled her more, and perhaps she might have done something about it, if she were not both preoccupied by the Cal clones and constrained by her word to keep her nose clean.

Dr. Mish had been especially interested in the clones, analyzing the copies of Cal Shemzak to ascertain how the Jaxdron had manufactured them. He admitted reluctantly that there were elements involved in their structure which, while apparently innocuous enough, were a mystery to him and significantly more complex than his squad of robots named after famous military leaders. It had been his voice that had quieted the strong suggestions that these copies be destroyed, in case they were dangerous. Here, he claimed, was the handiwork of the Jaxdron which might present clues as to their science, perhaps even their natures. Why toss this chance away, especially when there was no indication whatsoever that they were dangerous?

As for her promise to be loyal to the *Starbow*, its crew, and its cause, Laura had to consider something she'd experienced before. With duty to the Federation, it wasn't a matter of loyalty; it was conditioning and lack of choice. When she had thrown her lot in with this curious bunch of her own free will, something seemed to shift within her, aligning on a course that made her feel as if she were part of something special, not simply alone and struggling for her own survival.

It made her feel good, more whole. It gave her an intimation of the reason for society, much as her promises to Cal had given her a feeling of family, a notion the Federation abhorred.

The *Starbow* crew was a family of sorts, and that notion appealed to her. Families seemed to be important and valuable in the universe, yet hard to achieve and maintain. Families seemed a heritage from the past, a stepladder to the future; but most of all they seemed a cooperative way of dealing with that very strange and troublesome period—the present.

Beyond all that, there seemed to be an emptiness inside her that could only be filled by other people. Her early years had been filled with Cal, her brother; but then, when they were separated, she tried to tell herself that she needed no one, not even Cal; that she was self-reliant and hard and cold through and through; that what was left of her softer, more vulnerable emotions had been thoroughly protected and assigned to her caring for her brother.

Now, though, Laura was starting to have positive feelings about other people. It frightened her, dredging up cold memories of aloneness, isolation.

Captain Northern had picked up on this thawing of Laura's attitude, and while sharing coffee the morning before their arrival at Kendrick's Vision, he had commented on it.

"When you jumped aboard our ship, my dear, you were one brawly, feisty lady—even when your fur wasn't wet." He looked at her thoughtfully, coffee steam hazing his eyes, particularly greenish now. "You've calmed down quite a bit. I didn't know you had this kind of reserve in you."

Laura grinned. "Reserve? Goddammit, what do you mean by that? Just because I'm not so aggressive?"

Northern leaned back in his chair, his face assuming a calm, relaxed blankness. "Well, you're certainly letting us see another side of your character, you must admit that. Actually, I think we're good for you."

"What's that supposed to mean?" she said, bridling, on guard instantly.

His expression grew warmer and Laura was again amazed at the man's quixotic, surprising qualities. He was a chameleon of moods, and yet this calm openness registered as quite sincere. "It's like that aboard this ship, Laura. It's not just you. In the past year we've acquired perhaps seven or eight new crew members, and they've had experiences similar to yours."

"How do you know what my experiences here are?" Laura demanded, though without rancor. "Have you got some sort of mind-reader?"

"Oh, no. It's just that when we encounter most of the people who eventually become part of our number, they tend to be suspicious, cold individuals, as you were. You see, we all tend to assume at most parts of our lives that we're lonely victims of a cold, unfeeling universe." Casually, the Captain gazed off at the lounge's panoramic window, which showed a spectacular image of a nebula: a shower of stars, bathed in bold white, crimson, and cerulean. "And who can blame us? But you see, when as a group we see that we all feel this way, it becomes a kind of bond. Despite the variety of experiences and character idiosyncrasies, the wealth of common experience, shared experience, gives the very comforting and moving feeling of oneness and purpose. It's quite fulfilling, and I expect that you're feeling something of that, and I'm happy you are because you are certainly a welcome addition to the bunch."

Laura eyed him suspiciously. "Why do I get the distinct impression you're being condescending?"

"Who? Me?" Northern cried in mock alarm, his expression unreadable again.

"I just don't get you, Northern. Sometimes you're real friendly, sometimes you're not. Sometimes you play games, sometimes you don't. What gives, anyway?"

Northern chuckled sadly. "Moods, Laura. Perhaps just moods." He stood and made a dramatic sweep of his arm. "Or perhaps I like the concept of roles. All the worlds are stages, and I'm a repertory actor, mayhap." His face clouded over. "And then again, Laura Shemzak, perhaps I just don't know, and perhaps you shouldn't even ask."

Laura shrugged and saluted. "Whatever you say, great

leader. I'm not that intrigued, anyway.''

She was, but she wasn't going to divulge any of her feelings to this joker, she thought angrily. Deep inside, though, she wished she could, and pushed that thought back immediately.

"I hope you won't need me for your bar stop on this Kendrick's Vision place, because I have other things to do," she said grumpily.

"I had no intention of asking you, my dear," Northern said, smiling again at the mention of the word bar. "I know how you feel on the subject of our quest for your missing brother, but I assure you, it will all work out for the best in the end."

That was debatable, Laura thought, gloom descending. Nothing ever really worked out the way you hoped it would. You just had to grit your teeth and take whatever life tossed your way, using whatever ways possible to cushion the blows.

As she left the room, she absently touched the place on her abdomen that concealed her drug dispenser. Everybody had to have something, she thought. Captain Northern has his drink . . . and I have my—

A light shudder passed through her, but she shrugged it off.

Laura was in the room with the two Cal clones when the *Starbow* reached Kendrick's Vision, passing through its guard satellites using a code reserved just for its private visits. She was having a very pleasant three-way game of cards with them, chatting amicably about the past and possible futures, when Captain Northern, along with Silver Zenyo and Crewman Arbst Nichol shuttled down to the planet's surface.

It was about this time that the *Starbow* contingent on Kendrick's Vision ran into their trouble, the Cal clones beginning to mutate into what they really were.

Chapter Fifteen

Tars Northern never tired of planetfall. Now, as he piloted the shuttle down toward the brown and gray continent that held Shiva, capital city to Kendrick's Vision, two crew members by his side in shock chairs, he relished the roller-coaster sensations, the swaths of color and exhilaration. He wondered if this was how Laura Shemzak must feel in her blip-ship; a sense of abandon combined with a simultaneous joy of riding something almost alive.

The fact that he was going to see a friend made it all the more fun.

"Whoo-eee!" he said, dipping the boat's nose at a steeper angle than necessary. The force shield glowed red from friction with the thin atmosphere. An extra half G slammed the riders back into their sensor cushions.

Silver Zenyo cursed in a most indelicate manner for such a delicate-looking lady. "Northern, what are you trying to do, make this shuttle into a kitchen appliance?"

"Can't I have a little fun, Silver? It's not very often that I get out, you know." His eyes flicked her way a moment. "Sorry if I mussed your hair. I know you want it nice for Freeman."

That was the principal reason Silver had asked to come along. She and Freeman Jonst had enjoyed a romantic alliance the last time the *Starbow* had stopped at Kendrick's Vision. Not that she would have time to indulge herself in anything heavy this visit; their time was too short. But Northern knew that she did want to see him. She had considered staying on Kendrick's Vision with him last year; Northern was not sure why she hadn't.

Silver Zenyo was an odd one. The ship's mystery woman, Northern liked to call her. That she was beautiful no one could deny. She had a blend of smooth and sharp in her features that struck one first with their form, then barbed the gazer upon her mascara-dark eyes, like depthless jewels a-twinkle from their own peculiar lights within. With the captain's permission, she had designed a variation of the neutral gray epauletted basic uniform of the *Starbow* crew. Hers had red trim and tucks and creases emphasizing her slender, perfectly proportioned body. Her hair, a beautiful wealth of blond curls, was more an explicit part of her statement than a mere frame or ornament to her features.

One sexy lady, Northern thought, but he'd steered well clear. There was a danger in her eyes besides the mystery. True, this was part of her intriguing erotic flavor. Northern liked his danger as much as the next adventurer. No, the danger was more a kind of controlled frenzy inside her, a hunger for something that was not innocent, which seemed all-consuming.

Still, despite his misgivings, Northern found the woman to be an exceptionally competent, sometimes even brilliant, crew member. It was Silver Zenyo who masterminded the methodology of vessel looting. She programmed the robots to be quick and effective—and often went along, seemingly for the joy of it.

Silver Zenyo claimed she was from Beta Canopus, where the Federation had actually stepped in and squashed the independence of the Mendric colony because of the strategic qualities of the planet, and because it was within easy swatting distance. Her story was that she had stolen a ship and become an independent merchant and occasional pirate among the trade of the Free Worlds, limiting her piracy to Federation vessels. She had encountered Northern when her ship, the *Princeling*, and the *Starbow* were both preying upon the same Federation trader, a particularly ripe plum laden with exotic spices. The *Princeling* had run afoul of the trader's modern defense array; Northern had rescued her, wondering how the hell a solitary woman in a Class Five Scout could wage an effective pirate career. A lengthy interview answered that question: she was a hardware expert who knew the ins and outs of every Federation vessel, be it trader or fighter, like a top medical doctor knew the human body. She knew how to open one up quick and suck out the juice. In other words, she was just so damned good that Northern had to change his notion about setting her down on the nearest Free World to make her own way; she was too blasted valuable to let her slip through his fingers.

So, despite the vagueness of her background story, he asked her to become a crew member of the *Starbow*. Her apprenticeship was spectacularly successful; and so she was asked to stay on. Which she did because, she said, she could fight the Federation this way . . . and lay up a nice store of wealth for her declining years. Buy some planet, she said; have enough loot to buy her own beautiful paradise. She was a good officer, loyal, tart, and cool, and she did her job well.

But there was something more to her—something she wasn't coughing up—and while it always intrigued Northern, no one had found out if she indeed was hiding anything. Silver, after all, seemed a good and faithful member of their motley family. Her mystery was merely her particular idiosyncrasy, perhaps. Everyone had their private secrets. God knows I've got enough of them, Northern thought.

He turned his attention fully upon the exhilarating but tricky piloting of their shuttle down to the surface of Kendrick's Vision. Maybe good old Freeman would know more.

The flowery scent of Silver's perfume teased him all the way down.

When they neared Shiva, Northern turned to Arbst Nichol, who manned the navigational sensors and was a fantastic lander of shuttles in various sorts of non-spaceport terrain. "What have we got on those coordinates I threw you?"

The curly haired fellow turned his sunken eyes toward Northern. "Pretty good memory, Captain. It seems to be some kind of mansion all right, on the outskirts of the town. Got a nice field alongside it too. I'm going to be able to set this baby down pretty as you please!"

"Don't thank me, Arbst." Northern grinned over at their female companion. "Silver is the one that has all the details of Shiva and its president burned into her brain."

Silver Zenyo gave a lemon-twist of a smile but said nothing, keeping her attention upon her sensor board.

With the ease Arbst Nichol predicted, they set down on retros and repulsers in a grassy field beyond a ridge which hid the president's mansion from their view.

"Why didn't we radio down first, Captain?" Nichol wanted to know.

"It's a little game Freeman and I play from time to time," Northern returned mischievously. "Little surprises of various sorts. He's not going to be expecting me and the way was clear. Why not just drop in unannounced!"

Nichol's chubby features bent into a frown. "I don't know, Captain," he said doubtfully.

"Silver, anything amiss on the sensors?"

"Nothing I can ascertain, sir," Silver answered in a non-committal voice. She seemed preoccupied—no doubt with anticipation, Northern surmised.

"Well then," he said cheerily. "You will do us the favor of staying on board while we go and have a chat with old Freeman, won't you?"

"I presume that's an order," said Nichol. "Forgive me, sir, but sometimes I can't tell."

"Yes indeed. An order. Stand by, though, we're going to be needing your help in stowing some stuff on board."

"Aye aye, sir," Nichol said, swiveling around and pecking out instructions on a keyboard. "Opening procedures under way. Have a nice visit, sir."

The airlock began to open. The ladder descended onto the grassy sward beneath. Northern, followed by Zenyo, stepped out into the clean, fresh air of Kendrick's Vision; Northern was immediately reminded why he liked this place so much. Something about the atmosphere—faintly higher oxygen content, perhaps—something special that plants added, maybe. Whatever it was, it was relaxing and it was good. The stars twinkled overhead through a stirring of clouds. Insects made chittering noises in the nearby wood.

"Ah, the Vision," said Northern as the pair began to climb the rise. "Pardon my continual snoopiness, Silver, but I still can't figure out why you wanted to leave this place. It's as good as any to settle down in, isn't it, and you seemed to take quite a shine to Jonst . . . more than I've ever seen you take to anyone, come to think of it . . . and you do tend to do well with men, you can't deny that. If I were you—"

"You forget so easily, Tars Northern," Silver said, stopping, placing her hands on her hips, silhouetted by one of the small, greenish moons just rising from the horizon. "Sometimes I wonder if it's simply the way your mind works, or if your brain's eroding from your penchant for drink. Not one of us on that beautiful ship out there is normal in the slightest. We're all haunted, all driven. That's the common denominator. Now I realize that you've gotten this bee in your bonnet about commitment and family and somesuch rot, and maybe I agree—it's nice to have people around. Sure. But I'm a loner, Northern, just like you. My head is full of stuff beyond expression—haunted, just like that incredible, creaky old thing inside your head is. I've got things driving me that maybe even I don't understand. But what I do know is that I'm not about to settle down into a complacent, quiet life no matter how pleasant it might be, when I know that there are struggles occurring in this universe that I might take part in. I almost resent the fact that you think I'm different from you in that way. That's why we're together, Northern. That's why we're a crew. We're all dedicated to something, and that's our lives."

Northern grinned. "Just checking. I just thought that you dressed and looked your best to catch yourself a man sometime, and I can't think of more of a man than Freeman Jonst."

It was Silver's turn to smile, and in the light from the two moons and the running lights of their shuttle, Tars Northern could see that it was a gentle smile. "Tars, what else can I say except that a girl's just got to do what she can."

They topped the rise and found themselves looking down into a valley holding a sprawling Spanish-style villa. Lights shone in curtain windows. There were no guards. No reason for guards, here on Kendrick's Vision, a new colony where people were too busy working to build their dream to become criminals or to overthrow the government by assassinating the president.

"Too early for the old fellow to be in bed," said Northern. "He might be in his office. Do you remember where that is, dear heart?"

"Sure. Around this way. Your ploy of allowing Nichol to land seems to have worked. We came down so quietly with that sensor cloak, nobody seems to know that we're here."

"I owe that pal of yours a surprise and I can't think of a better way of giving him one than to walk in unannounced with you." He could feel his face getting a devilish expression on it. "I don't suppose you might consider going in bare-assed, would you?"

"You really have too nice a face to take such risks of getting it marked up, Northern. Come on, it's over here."

They crept up along a hedgerow to a window and peered in.

A man with graying, bushy hair was poring intently over something at his desk. He was dressed in plain khaki coveralls and wore spectacles. Freeman Jonst, working.

"Through the window?" Northern suggested in a whisper.

"That's a bit much, Captain, don't you think? I mean, Freeman generally carries a gun—that's part of his philosophy, you remember, and if he sees a couple of legs come cruising through his side window, he's likely to shoot first and ask for names later."

"Right you are. I knew there were reasons beyond your fabulous beauty that I keep you on my ship. Now as I recall, there's a door hereabouts."

There was, and they found it without much problem, walking into a tastefully decorated hallway done in a curious mixture of old Earth styles. Freeman Jonst had always been fascinated with the more leisurely cultures of old Earth, particularly the Latin, and had utilized much of his architectural penchants on his vital and growing colony.

Tars Northern had met the man not long after he had stolen the *Starbow*. He knew of the reputation of Kendrick's Vision as a hold-out of individualism amongst even the Free Worlds. He thought the planet worthwhile to investigate as part of his efforts to rally independent planets together in a loose consortium designed to repulse any Federation efforts to regain territory.

They had met, and although Jonst had not been interested in the consortium idea, he had taken to the unpredictable Northern. They'd become fast friends and drinking buddies. Northern had been given the planetary equivalent of the key to the city and often traveled back to Kendrick's Vision to trade supplies, sell stolen loot, pick up booze, or simply pay a visit, always knowing he was welcome, always knowing that he and his crew were safe there. The Vision was so far away from Federation space that its area had virtually no Federation traffic; thus the *Starbow* could feel at ease.

So Kendrick's Vision was like a planetary vacation spot for Tars Northern. If he had anything approaching a planetary home now, this was it. *"Mi casa es su casa,"* Freeman Jonst had said, and if any man could be taken at his word, it was his friend Freeman.

Voices muttered in the distance. There was the scent of fresh wood and wax in the air, a good smell. Sometimes when he came down to places like this, Northern realized that even as committed as he was to the *Starbow* and its crew, and as much as he belonged to the starways, he missed the feel, touch, and taste, the security, of living on a planet's surface.

Silver indicated a door and Northern followed her.

The door was open. The pair strode in as casually as they might if they lived in the place.

The man at the desk stopped writing something and looked up at them. He blinked. His jaw dropped a bit.

"Hallo, Jonsty, old friend," said Northern. "We were just passing town and thought we'd drop in for a visit.

"Hello, Freemen," said Silver in a soft, breathy voice.

Tars Northern had never seen his friend at such a loss for words. Freeman sputtered and choked and his eyes grew big and then he finally coughed out: "What in God's name are you—" A terrified look appeared on his face. "Get out! Get out right now!"

Northern stepped forward, surprised. "What's wrong, Freeman?"

"I get the feeling," said Silver Zenyo in her normal voice, "that we really should have radioed first."

The door squeaked behind them. Freeman Jonst's eyes flicked to the new arrival.

Northern and Zenyo spun around.

Standing in the doorway was an overweight man, immaculately dressed in high station Federation uniform, his prissy, self-satisfied expression combined with a smile of eager delight.

"Well, well, well," the man said, lifting a gun. "How constantly surprised I am by the vagaries of chance," said Overfriend Zarpfrin. "Greetings and well met, Tars Northern. We've a few things to discuss, I think."

Chapter Sixteen

Laura was just about to leave them when the clone twins began to change.

They had just finished a pleasant game of cards featuring high spirits of the Cal kind. Puns and jokes flew, one or the other mimicking famous characters, pure silliness of the sort that the original Cal could be so good at, with a unique intensity borne of playing off himself.

The banter and antics amused Laura so much that for the moment she forgot her impatience with their stop-off in this system. Still, though, she wanted to run a check on her blip-ship. As they had agreed, Northern's bunch was doing an analysis of the craft, and she wanted to make sure they hadn't knocked anything out of whack.

She had said her farewells to the pair and was at the open door when one of them, she didn't know which, called out, "Oh, and Laura, just one more thing!"

Laura spun on a heel, expecting some finale to their escapades. A silly face, a raspberry, a head stand—anything but what confronted her. Cal One and Cal Two stood, their arms joined together in a grotesque mass of shifting, greenish protoplasm.

"What the hell are you doing!" The sentence ended with a shriek.

Their faces had grown rigid, their eyes glassy and vacant, focused on infinity. The bubbling mass of protoplasm spread up to the shoulders and dripped down the chest, translucent enough to show metamorphizing activity. Flesh and bone and electronics were becoming—something else!

"Laura! Laura Shemzak!" they said, their voices blending together into a weird buzz. "Transmission established at optimum moment! Units functioning as programmed. A successful ploy in the minor arcana of strategem! Field impulsers and limited theta module power dictate immediate action after mobile unit achieves ambulatory wholeness."

"I'm getting someone to take a look at you guys!" Laura said, more than a bit unnerved at this sight.

Suddenly, their eyes focused upon her. Already their heads were joined. They looked like Siamese twins melting into some ungodly horror. "No, Laura Shemzak. The life of your brother is at risk. Hamper this move and surely he shall suffer pain beyond your imagining!"

"The Jaxdron!" Laura said, feeling paralyzed. "I'm actually talking to— You goddamn bunch of wretches! What do you think you're doing? Let me have my brother back!"

"Ah, then, our readings on you are accurate. A very simple emotional matrix of priorities. How delightfully and outrageously primitive. Oh, the joys of manipulation!" The mouths had grown together by now, the voice had become single. "But stay, Laura Shemzak, for we wish you no harm, and we have word of your brother, whom we hold in captivity."

"No kidding, jerks! And I'm going to get him back!"

"Please forgive us our lack of variety in the vocabulary of your language, and make your messages simple."

"I thought that was simple enough! Can you let me talk to Cal?"

"Your brother is being most cooperative and is quite comfortable, Laura Shemzak. He is indeed upon the planet we indicated most melodramatically to the adept one of your crew. Oh, the joys of intimidation! Yes, yes, and you come to save him, but the others . . . the other humans and non-human have other needs, yes, yes? They care very little for the fate of Cal Shemzak."

"But he's safe, you haven't rotted his mind? Why did you duplicate him, why all this weirdness?"

"Oh, curious creature, we can only know bits and pieces of transtextural reality, and we have time only for small pieces. Oh, the delights of war, the intrigues of strategy! The extratemporal energies involved in this transmission are outrageous and we must be on our way. Now lead on, Laura Shemzak, for our unit is nearing readiness."

The two bodies had indeed become one oozing mass of protoplasm, still transforming into some as yet undetermined form.

"That's why you left the clones!" Laura said. "A pair of Trojan horses! But I can't let you do harm to this ship or any of its crew members!"

"Oh, be advised that no harm is intended now and is not the purpose of the unit in formation. We seek only to uncover a secret of the *Starbow* . . . a secret you might well have use of yourself, Laura Shemzak. Forgive our threats concerning your brother, but truly it is not in his best interests to have the crew apprised of our activities."

Laura swallowed. "What do you want me to do?"

The newly created organism—only vaguely humanoid, with eyes that seemed to glow with phosphoresence, with skin that still moiled like a fretful puddle surface covering twinkling diodes, twisting wires—stood unsteadily.

"There is a place at the hub of the radiating spokes that extends from the middle of this vessel—a place that is off-limits to all the crew save the captain, and of course the curious creature known as Dr. Michael Mish. You know of this place."

Laura did. "There's a lot of places that are off-limits, but they're not going to want to let a Jaxdron-controlled beastie in there! And I'm not sure I want you there either."

"The screams of your brother can be transmitted here easily, Laura Shemzak. Cal is easily obtainable and our methods of torture are exquisite."

"Okay, okay," said Laura, resigned. How could she notify the crew of what was happening here? She couldn't do anything. She prayed that Dr. Mish was watching this and had something ready for this thing that the replicates of Cal had become. "But don't expect me to help you beyond that."

"Oh, do not worry," said the thing, its hide thickening and opaque. "There is a reason for you being there as well, Laura Shemzak. Hail, O blessed strategy! Now my form is complete and ready, and the time is optimum."

Almost as punctuation to the creature's prophesy, the red alert klaxon sounded from down the hallway.

"They've found you out!" Laura said.

"Oh, no, no. Sensors show that the *Starbow* has an entirely different dilemma which shall occupy its attention and its crew's attention. This is why this moment was chosen. We are quite a bit less than stupid. Now please, time is valuable. We must go."

Laura had no choice but to obey the thing.

But beneath her fear for her brother and for the well-being of this ship, there was a genuine curiosity.

She was going to find something out about the *Starbow*'s secrets!

Chapter Seventeen

Captain Tars Northern looked from the bore of Overfriend Zarpfrin's gun to the stunned expression on the face of Freeman Jonst. "So, I see you've got rodent problems here on the Vision, President. May I suggest a good exterminator?"

"May I suggest that right now you divest yourself of your weapons, Tars Northern," Zarpfrin said, "or I shall exercise my exterminating privileges?"

Both Zenyo and Northern eased their pistols from their holsters and dropped them on the ground.

"Northern, you must understand, there was no other choice," Freeman Jonst said. "I had to call them in to protect us from the Jaxdron."

"Sounds like the foxes guarding the henhouse, Jonst," said Northern.

"I didn't ask you to come here, dammit! I would have warned you away!" Jonst met Silver Zenyo's glare, then turned his wrinkle-wreathed eyes away.

"I had hoped you might drop in and visit here sometime, Northern, but I had no idea it would be so soon!" Zarpfrin said. "As for your comment, I have assured President Jonst that the Federation's military presence here in this system is solely to protect human interests in the Jaxdron war. Once this terrible threat is contained, we shall go, asking only continued relations, such as trading, to keep our bonds of humanity tight. We have even signed treaties here to assure one another of good faith. However, there is nothing in these treaties to prevent us from dealing out justice to criminals who happen to stop by unannounced. Now, if you'll excuse me, please remain very still while I call in some help. I'm not so stupid as to think I can handle you alone, Northern. You're much too slippery."

He lifted a communicator from his belt and thumbed open a channel. "Yes, Hodgkins, if you would, send about five fully armed security officers to the president's office by aircar. We've a pair of interesting intruders. Oh yes, and punch in full alert on our spacecraft for Wanted Vessel, Specs 4325A . . . Starbow. We've got its captain down here, so it must be somewhere up there. I'd be very pleased if we could capture it, but if we can't, feel free to destroy it. Over."

He placed the communicator back and smiled warmly. "Now then, Captain, you know it might go better with you if you help us get the Starbow. Spare your crew—things like that. So why don't you simply cooperate?"

Northern shook his head and returned Zarpfrin's smile. "You know I couldn't do that." He strode nonchalantly toward the liquor cabinet. "You don't trust me and I don't trust you. We've been wonderful enemies, Zarpfrin, and I don't know of any good reason why that should not continue just as long as possible." He poured himself a drink. "Mind if I carry along a couple bottles of this stuff, Freeman? It's one of my favorites."

"Get away from there, man!" said Zarpfrin, raising his voice. "Has that stuff rotted your brain? I've got a gun on you. I can shoot you on the spot!"

"Oh, maybe, but somehow I very much doubt it, Zarpfrin. Sometime you'll want me dead—or at the very least, sucked out and erased. But for right now, I would venture to say that you've got your gun on stun."

"A little more power than that. I'd prefer to have you conscious and undamaged, Northern, but if necessary—"

Silver Zenyo was still looking at Freeman Jonst. "I still don't understand how you could sell out," she said.

"Two weeks ago," Jonst said, averting their eyes, "the Jaxdron broke through our defenses and laid waste to a large portion of our capital. The attack was devastating—but more devastating was with what ease they accomplished it . . . and the implicit promise that a larger force would be back to deal out further decimation. To see all we've worked for so long, destroyed by a bunch of faceless aliens . . . it was too much. Zarpfrin is right, Silver. Blood will out. When it comes to a clinch, humans must unite."

"No, no, something is very wrong here," Silver said, shaking her blond locks emphatically. "Can't you see it, Freeman? Or have they got control of you, riddled you with their puppet strings until you're just jerking about at the twitching of their bent fingers?"

"This really is getting to be a bit much," said Zarpfrin wearily. "I've had enough of your traitorous ways, Tars Northern. I am moved by the ultimate loyalty of President Jonst to his people and to humanity. Ideas are fine, but our first duties are to the race, no? And your perverse ways have led you to prey on that race, Tars Northern. Now, if you would—"

Suddenly, Zarpfrin's gun was blasted from his grasp. The Overfriend yelped and instinctively pulled his hand back, rubbing it as he stared, shocked, at President Freeman Jonst.

"This doesn't change our deal, Zarpfrin," Jonst said. "If I wanted that, your head would be all over the wall. I didn't expect my friends to drop in, though, and while I'm a damned faithful leader, I'm also a faithful friend." Keeping his gun trained on the nonplussed Zarpfrin, he turned to Zenyo and Northern. "Now would you two get your asses out of here before that security detachment arrives?"

Tars Northern saluted. "I knew you wouldn't let us down, Freeman. Just so this trip isn't entirely wasted . . ." He grabbed a full bottle of rare Cognac from the top of the table. "And watch out for this snake here." They both scooped up their guns. Northern grinned at his adversary. "I should take this opportunity to do what I should have done a long time ago, Zarpfrin. But in honor of my friend Jonst here, I won't."

"I'll make you wish you had, Tars Northern," Zarpfrin said. "I promise you that."

"We'll be back sometime to liberate Kendrick's vision, Jonst," said Northern. "Meantime, enjoy your enslavement." He indicated to Silver Zenyo that this time the window was appropriate.

"Well see about that!" Freeman Jonst called after them. Zarpfrin made a move, but the president of Kendrick's Vision quickly realigned the sights of his gun and said, "I wouldn't do that, Overfriend. Until they get clear of here, consider our agreement suspended. I must say, if you happen to get shot, I'm sure that the Federation has someone to replace you, so don't tempt me."

"They won't get away!" Zarpfrin cried. "They can't. I've alerted all my forces here. Why throw in with them, Jonst, when they are the losers?"

"A temporary aberration, let's say. But for right now, just stay where you are and we shall have a negotiating session. There are some aspects of our deal which I realize now don't quite suit me."

Zarpfrin fumed.

Chapter Eighteen

"Oof!" said Silver as she fell off the porch.

Tars Northern just missed catching her. He helped her up. "C'mon, hurry! God knows when that security aircar is going to show up."

"I broke two nails!" Silver said disgustedly, studying her hands.

"Just get moving now, woman," Northern said, grabbing her arm and pulling her. They began to run up the slope, toward the shuttle.

However did this happen? Northern wondered. I must remember not to take *anything* for granted! But at least it was good for some exercise!

Not sixty yards into their upward sprint, a pair of headlights pricked their way around the side of Jonst's hacienda. A roar. A jabber of voices.

"Oh, well," said Northern. "So much for a clean escape!"

Silver turned her head and saw the sleek outline of the aircar making its way in an exploratory fashion around the side of the building. A searchlight stabbed through the ground mist, as a voice yelled instructions from the porch. They realized that Freeman Jonst must have been relieved of his tactical position and now they were on their own.

"No time for gawking, let's move it!" Northern instructed in a harsh voice.

Silver Zenyo needed no further encouragement.

The searchlight played over the grassy slope as the hovering aircar began to move toward them. Northern could hear the squeak of a gun turret as the security men sought them out. Idly he wondered if the set was full blast or stun, and knew he'd get his answer very soon.

Their breaths were harsh in their throats as their feet stamped up the long slope, legs whipping through the grasslike vegetation which formed a kind of lawn for the estate. The wild, fresh scents of the night swept about Tars Northern, a reminder of the life it was his duty to cling to.

I can't die nor let them get me, his mind raged. I must complete what has been begun. The thought urged his body to a new speed. Silver Zenyo struggled to keep up, her immaculate hairdo now a mess.

The searchlight flicked their way as the aircar hummed nearer. A sliver of light caught Silver, casting a shadow. A cry of victory, a hiss of heat cutting through the dark, a zapping of intense light as it danced along the ground just short of their feet: the blaster was not set on stun.

Silver yelped and Northern swung his gun around and squeezed off a spurt of fire which went wide of its mark.

"Separate," he ordered. "Zigzag up the slope!"

He lunged away from her, rolling through the damp grass then into a kneel. He took a careful bead this time and put out the searchlight in an explosion of glass and the clap of a vacuum filling. But Northern's fire placed him. Blaster fire answered his pistol work, searing a mere meter short, singeing the hair on Northern's arm. He leaped away and rolled, then dug his feet back into the ground and ran for all he was worth.

Orders were shouted in the car and it leaped toward them, blaster kicking up gouts of flaming turf as it roared after Northern.

One of the Vision's moons was rising on the other side of the slope, providing a soft new light. Northern could see Silver's silhouette rising up into that light, a perfect target.

"Silver!" he yelled. "Get down!"

The fiery line of light stabbed out just as the woman obeyed. But it caught her on one side, and she shrieked.

Like a beast sensing a kill, the aircar snorted toward its victim. Northern lifted his gun and tried to fire but it was jammed.

The aircar approached the crest of the hill, closing in—

And was suddenly blasted, tail over rotors, by fire from atop the slope. The Federation security officers were thrown from the car as it crashed and crumpled down the slope.

Northern spun around. A figure holding a rifle stood beyond him. "I know you said not to leave the shuttle, Captain," said Arbst Nichol. "But I just got some terrible news from the *Starbow* and figured you might be in trouble."

"That's one way of putting it," Northern said grimly as he strode over to where Silver Zenyo lay in the pale moonlight. She sat up clutching her upper arm as he approached, "Got a bandaid?" she asked.

Northern grinned with relief. "Bit of a moontan, huh? Easy there, lady." He helped her up. "Talk about getting burned in love."

"Please, Northern," she said as they hobbled back to the shuttle, Nichol covering them should any of the Federation folk rise up from unconsciousness. "Spare me the bad jokes and get me to the med cabinet for some nice dermaplast."

They made their way to the shuttle very quickly. "You would have thought we'd have seen Federation troops!" Arbst Nichol commented.

"Uh-uh, too few," said Northern as he helped Zenyo up the ramp. "This is just a parlay expedition."

"With two destroyer-class starships out there?" Nichol said as he pounded up after them, drawing the ramp up after him.

"I'm sure that all Overfriends travel well-protected," said Silver, stumbling her way toward the medical compartment, her pretty face contorted with pain. "I'll be all right here, you two just get us back to the *Starbow*. I foresee a rough flight."

"And what is Thur's report?" Northern inquired grimly.

"Right now they're attempting an evasive maneuver, sir. Our rendezvous point is at the same coordinates as departure point."

"If we can make it up there in time," said Zenyo, "and if they don't have much trouble with those destroyers."

"What? The *Starbow*?" Northern laughed as the shuttle lifted on wings of force and shot up through the night sky. "My pretty boat is more than a match for any pair of Feddy rust buckets!"

"Judas Priest," cried Akrm Thur, picking himself up off the floor. "What was that?" He recovered his aplomb immediately as he reassumed the captain's chair and barked out orders for status reports.

"The shields absorbed most of the explosion," said Gemma Naquist, who'd had the forethought of strapping herself in upon first sighting of the Federation ships.

"Sensors indicate a jump-missile, Thur," reported Dr. Mish. "Proton torpedo jacked up for a brief Underspace jump. Prohibitively expensive for battle purposes. They must really want us."

"Maximum impulse! Program an evasive course so jagged that they can't plot where we'll be if they're thinking about sending us another of those babies!"

The Federation cruisers could go no faster than the *Starbow*—but they could keep up, occasionally flicking out power beams when the pi-merc vessel cut off some of its distance with an abrupt change of course. They both were following the *Starbow* and Akrm Thur figured that was good just as long as there wasn't some other Federation ship skulking about, ready to pounce either on the *Starbow* or the shuttle bearing the captain. But sensors indicated no such ship. The Federation was throwing all its force now at the *Starbow*. Just what I need today, thought First Mate Thur. A space chase.

After some minutes of this madness, heading out for a circumnavigation of the Vision's moon, Tether Mayz swung around in her chair and said, "We've got the captain on the line, sir. They'll be at interception point at twenty-three point two minutes."

"What?" Thur said. "Damn, forget about the moon, Jitt. We simply haven't got time! Plot us a course that will get us back to those coordinates in time."

Dansen Jitt did some speedy figuring. "Sir, the only way we can do that is to head right back through the enemy, after a tight curve that's going to put a lot of strain on the artificial gravity here, to say the least."

"Well, as Captain Northern might point out, that'll be the last thing they expect. Prepare proton torpedoes and beams. They're not going to know what hit them!"

"Aye aye, sir," his officers answered doubtfully but without question. The *Starbow* had done stranger things in its career.

Immediately, the vessel began to cut an arc that would in very short time bring it around full circle. However, the Federation cruiser stayed tight on its tail, following the course exactly, using the opportunity to rake the ship's force fields with their own lasers, albeit to little effect. The *Starbow* dropped a few torpedoes their way, only one of which seemed to have any effect.

"Officer Mayz, inform the captain and his pilot of our exact trajectory. We're going to have to grab them with a tractor beam and haul them aboard as we pass. I just hope the shuttle hull is going to be able to withstand the pressure because this is the only way."

Tether Mayz made the appropriate communication, waited for the response, then swung back to Thur. "Sir, the captain hopes you realize that this is going to be a golden first if we can pull it off."

Thur turned to Dr. Mish. "Just a moment. Doctor . . . that special beam you used on the Jaxdron . . . you think you might conjure up another one of those? That would do the trick, I think."

"Yes," said Dr. Mish, his face showing traces of unspoken trouble. "Yes, that could be arranged, and it would appear to be the best hope in the given situation. My resources have certainly recharged sufficiently. Only—"

"Only what, Doctor?" said Arkm Thur. How strange to realize that when you spoke to Dr. Mish, you were actually speaking to *Starbow* itself. "That torpedo we caught give you an upset stomach?"

"An appropriate analogy, Thur," said Dr. Mish. He blinked. "Something wrong . . . deep within." He closed his eyes and spoke lower. "I have been . . . the core . . . my Heart . . . the Portal. Intruders!" He opened his eyes again. "I must leave."

The construct sat down and relaxed into oblivion.

Arkm Thur ran over and shook the body violently. No response. "Damn," he said, checking the chronometer. "If he doesn't get this problem fixed in ten minutes, we're going to be in deep trouble!"

"Going to be?" Dansen Jitt said as he looked up at the rear vu-screen depicting the cruisers coming after them like brimstone-breathing demons from Hell.

"Did anybody find Laura Shemzak yet?" the First Mate demanded.

Nobody had.

Chapter Nineteen

To begin with, it looked like no room that Laura Shemzak had ever seen—in or out of a starship.

There was no furniture per se, only a few blocks strewn on the floor in a peculiar pattern. A thick mist moved about these like amorphous ectoplasm, pulsing with all manner of lights. The air seemed to vibrate with light from the tubular lights that veined a fibrous wall. In the center of the room was a series of columns attached ceiling to floor, the stones resembling a cross between a Greek temple and Stonehenge. They formed a huge boxlike room of their own. On one side Laura could see wirelike apparatus, on another a dark rectangular mirror of obsidian which caught the lights flowing through the room and reflected them back in mystical hues.

"Come, Laura Shemzak, and behold a prize beyond imagining," said the Jaxdron creature. "We had reason to believe that this almost mystical structure was the center, the secret of the *Starbow*, ever since we trained the analysis ray upon it and obtained hints. And so now we behold it truly, knowing that we must have it or its like."

"What is it?" Laura said, unable to keep her eyes from the weird, dazzling thing.

"It is one of the Relics of the Older Times, of the Elder Beings, Laura Shemzak. It is one of our R'nth'na—our Goal Mysteries. But we waste time talking. We must be about our purpose. Observe and ponder, lowly one."

The creature strode to the side of the glassy monolith, extending its fingers into delicate filaments which touched and stroked the coils and wires experimentally. "Heed, oh my brothers. Observe the Gate!"

Laura wanted to do something, anything, but she found herself in a curiously mesmerized state, watching as the sides of the box began to pulse their lights stronger, harder, like a beating heart filled with multicolored blood-light. Whether this Jaxdron monster meant the *Starbow* harm was not apparent. But it hadn't hurt her, had it? Besides, what could she do, beat on its back?

The creature's eyes were bright with inhuman satisfaction as its fingers lengthened again, weaving themselves through the webworking of the side. "Much to be learned!" it said. "Much to be explored! Much to win!" With its right limb it began to touch the glassy face, fingers pushing gently.

It stopped, seemingly vexed. "What is this? Our computers predict penetration at this point! Yet the side is as solid as—"

Suddenly the sides of the room began to rumble like the bowels of God Himself. A phantom wind swirled the mist violently. A thunder vibrated everything, and the light within this wondrous core room began to congeal into violently extended lightning bolts.

"The Guardian is alerted!" the Creature said. "Evacuate synoptic interceptors before transmission is reversed and—"

Sparks began to fly from where the creature's fingers touched the monolith.

The thing's eyes flew wide and it began to shake violently, its scream submerged within the furious roar of power surging through its body. Flames began to leap out of it, the odor of burnt flesh and circuitry drifting over to Laura, who covered her nose and turned to run.

The door slammed shut, barring her exit.

By now the Jaxdron creature was totally engulfed in fire. Somehow it pulled itself away from its entanglement, staggered back, then crumpled onto the floor not two meters from Laura. The mist closed in upon it, and Laura watched as the flames were doused by the fog. The burned body then began to decompose, leaving only its metalloplast components.

The wild throbbing of the central monolith diminished; the thunder softened to echoes. A voice which seemed to fill the entire chamber spoke; Laura recognized it immediately. It belonged to Dr. Michael Mish.

It was the ship's voice!

"Oh, excellent, excellent!" it said. "I had rather hoped that something like this might happen! A nice tap through to Jaxdron Central if I may say so myself. But such an inconvenient time!"

"Dr. Mish!" Laura said, breaking out of her spell. "Just what the hell is going on down here! Open the door and let me out of this accursed place, will you!"

"Oh yes, Laura Shemzak," said the voice of the *Starbow*, turning ominous. "It really is rather too bad you've found this place, isn't it?"

A strand of static electricity snapped around the border of the monolith like a white and jagged whip.

"Two minutes to interception point," said Arbst Nichol through a groan. They had all suffered from the extra G-force they took in their hurry to get up here, especially Silver, who was moaning back in the grav-couch. "Any let-up in that interference yet?"

Captain Tars Northern wiped a bit of blood off the side of his mouth and checked the radio again. Nothing. "Goddamn Feddies must be so close they're jamming all our frequencies."

The globe beneath them that was the planet Kendrick's Vision was rimmed on one edge with a brilliant and beautiful sunrise. Northern wished he had the time and the safety in which to enjoy the scenery.

"If they're chasing them, how are they going to stop and pick us up?" asked Nichol, clearly troubled.

"How much firepower have we got on this shuttle?"

"Well, we did take one of the boys armed for piracy ventures . . . the usual complement of lasers, a couple of missiles strapped to the side."

"Warm up the lasers, my lad. I think we might need them."

"But, sir, these are used on freighters and scouts and small cowardly class vessels, not on cruisers and destroyers and dreadnaughts!" said Nichol. "They'll be useless. And if we provoke fire from them . . . well, that'll be it."

"With the kind of orders Zarpfrin has no doubt given these guys, they're going to shoot anyway, so we might as well give them what we've got. Right, Zenyo?''

"That's okay, Northern. I think I want to die anyway.''

"Where the hell are they?'' Nichol complained, searching the starfield hopefully, then checking the sensors.

On board the bridge of the *Starbow* similar concerns were being expressed.

"Give me that again, Naquist,'' demanded Thur.

"Temporary loss of power in the impellors, sir,'' she said. "There was some sort of drain on the main cells!''

"Captain!'' called Dansen Jitt. "The Federation ships are right on our tail! Sensors read a preparation for a strong barrage!''

"Divert secondary power to rear force screen!'' Thur ordered, and no sooner had those screens been strengthened than the tandem cruisers unleashed a mighty stream of energy. The bridge shook and rattled tremendously, but this time all were securely strapped in, and there was only momentary confusion before the laser banks answered with a short volley of their own, which blew off a Federation nacelle.

"Damage report!'' Thur ordered.

"Nothing structural, sir, but we did lose an impellor bank.''

"Dammit, give me a burst of the liquid fuel rockets then!''

"Aye aye, sir.''

The blast resumed the previous distance between pursued and pursuer, but the Federation cruisers continued dogging the *Starbow*'s tail.

Meanwhile, the shuttle bearing Captain Northern and his fellows had established an orbit that maintained the rendezvous coordinates. Arbst Nichol's vigilance was finally rewarded first with sensor readings, then a visual track on the approaching starships screaming soundlessly toward them through space.

"Doesn't look good, Captain,'' said Nichol. "Hands on weapons, though. I think you're the more skilled pilot.''

"Yes. Just one moment please.'' Captain Northern dug through a bag and took a quick swig from the premium booze he'd snagged from Freeman Jonst's bar. "Right. Ready for rendezvous!''

Nichol nodded. "Yes, sir.''

On the bridge Gemma Naquist announced, "We've got them! They're where they should be! Four point three minutes until we're within rendezvous radius!''

"Dr. Mish!" cried Thur. "Wake up, fellow!"

Dr. Mish complied immediately. "Yes! Sorry for the absence—I'll explain later. What seems to be the situation?" he added brightly.

"Communications are still jammed," said Thur. "Federation ships are still dead on our tail. I suppose that Captain Northern knows enough to start a course paralleling our path, but we're going a lot faster than his shuttle is capable of. That super tractor-beam trick of yours will come in handy, but we sure could use a distraction for those Feddy ships to give us some breathing space."

"Oh, I've already arranged for that," said Dr. Mish. "In fact, just about now. . . ."

"Sir, we read activity on the Docking Bay Level!" said Gemma Naquist. "A vehicle exiting!"

"Ah, excellent," said Dr. Michael Mish with a whimsical smile. "That will be Laura and her XT, I believe. I found her, you see. And where she shouldn't be. But I thought it best to make sure that there is a future to deal with the matter."

He looked down at his sensor boards.

"Now then. That tractor beam, you say. Now just how did I do that?"

Chapter Twenty

She zipped into space, having attached herself in what must have been record time inside the blip-ship.

The first thing she saw was the pair of Federation cruisers headed straight for her like deadly bullets from a brace of guns.

She felt the instant rush of adrenaline and other less natural drugs enter her system, and immediately she was one with the situation, seeing instantly what she must do.

Employing the element of surprise, she streaked between the ships and with a truly pyrotechnic exercise of rays, blasted away the frontmost sensor pods of both.

She dodged the initial salvo of responding beams, spun about, and started working on the engines where the shields were at their weakest.

Thank heavens she knew her Federation hardware!

Reveling in the oneness she felt with the blip-ship, she dove and spun and cavorted through the crisscross of enemy fire, her own salvoes a masterwork of destructive surgery.

Then a beam grazed her and she was knocked away, momentarily dazed. She recovered and slammed out an impulser which drove her farther away, beyond accurate range of their power beams. She took the time to focus upon the *Starbow*.

Where was it?

Her berserker assault upon the Federation cruisers had

veered them off their course. Hurrah, she thought. Just what I promised Mish I would do.

But how much time had elapsed?

Then her sensors picked up the already distant readings of the *Starbow*.

She dodged a power beam, then tried to make radio contact: "XT Nine calling *Starbow*. XT Nine calling *Starbow*. Hey, you creeps aren't going to leave me, are you? You got Northern's ass safe now?"

"Roger, XT Nine. This is the *Starbow*," responded Tether Mayz's voice. "Commander Thur, we've got an open frequency! Laura's reporting."

Arkm Thur's voice erupted over the transmission.

"We've hauled him in Laura but if you could give us a couple minutes grace, we certainly would appreciate it."

"Hey," said Laura, noting the cruisers separating, one pursuing the *Starbow*, the other hanging back to deal with her, its offensive pods already glowing in preparation for battle with this incredibly powerful mosquito bugging it. "What you think I am, a one-woman fleet?"

"Your abilities surprise us constantly," said Thur. "Jitt, you do have those astrogation figures? Right. Laura, hold them for just four more minutes and then jump to these coordinates. That should give us just enough time to outdistance them and then we can jump ourselves."

He read off the coordinates and Laura duly noted them. "Right," she said. "I'll give it a go, but have those dock doors wide open for me. Over."

She sighed inwardly, waiting for her second breath. About her she could feel her energy, the crackle of her force fields, the hum of her waiting lasers, the touch of the never-ending spectacle of space.

Hell, she thought. I shouldn't complain so much. I enjoy this.

She banked and skipped blithely away from the Federation Cruiser looming her way and headed for the one striking after the *Starbow*.

She smiled to herself. There was nothing more vulnerable to fire than the rear end of a Feddy cruiser!

When Captain Tars Northern reached the bridge of the

Starbow, the crew was too busy to greet him with anything but the odd grunt. He took the opportunity to get his breath back.

When the ship was back up to proper acceleration, Arkm Thur breathed a sigh of relief and turned to his captain. "All yours, sir." He noticed that Northern was alone. "The others?"

"Arbst is taking Silver to sick bay. Bit of a wound to the arm." He assumed the abandoned captain's chair. "Status, Gentlepeople?"

Dr. Mish turned his eyes to the ceiling.

"That bad?"

"The doctor had a little problem," explained Naquist.

"Everything is in equilibrium now, Tars," said Dr. Mish. "But if I might bend your ear for a moment . . ."

"Nothing to do now but run," said Thur.

"Very well, Mish. What is it?"

Dr. Mish tugged him along into a side cubicle out of earshot of the rest of the crew.

"Our little addition to the crew has a definite penchant for going where she doesn't belong. . . . We're going to have to explain about the core."

After hours of cool in frightening situations, Captain Northern finally lost his composure. "What? How did she stumble in there?"

"You remember my suspicions about those replicates of Cal Shemzak?"

"Yes, like Trojan horses. But you were keeping them well monitored—"

"Correct, and it turned out to be worthwhile in the long run. But there were some tricky moments. The Jaxdron took the opportunity presented by the confusion here to meld the twins and find the core. They were dealt with and they have nothing now in knowledge they didn't have before. But they took Laura along for the ride, and she saw it. I promised to explain if she would immediately jump in her blip-ship and cover for us. But, dear boy, if we explain to her, we'll have to explain to everyone."

Tars Northern nodded, feeling more sober than he had ever felt before in his life. "It's just as well. This is a fine crew, Mish, and I've hated keeping these secrets about the very reasons for our existence from them. Now that we may be embarked upon the deciding adventure of our career . . ." He took a breath. "Yes, they will have to know, and then they can each decide if they want to stay on."

"I . . . I don't know if I can allow that option, Tars Northern! This is the reason for secrecy!"

"Look, we need a crew. Dammit, it's just going to be that way! If anyone doesn't like the situation, we'll just put them down somewhere they can't hurt us with the knowledge I give them. Mish, you're so close now. We'll have the time!"

"Yes," said Mish. "Perhaps you are right. Before, when we started, I perhaps would not have hesitated to take a human life between me and my goal. But over these years, Tars Northern . . . with this group, your family, my family, I have changed."

"Captain!" said First Mate Thur. "Come out here and look at this!"

Tars Northern looked at Dr. Mish. "Every day, my friend, I am more and more sure that I did the right thing by casting my fate to your wind." Impulsively, he hugged the construct, and it was like hugging a brother.

Dr. Mish returned the hug awkwardly. "You must forgive me, Tars, I am not familiar with these feelings."

"C'mon, my friend, let's go see what Thur is screaming about."

Thur pointed up to the vu-screen. "She's a total maniac, sir! I wouldn't like to have that woman and her blip-ship come after me!"

The screen presented the image of the Federation cruiser struggling with its small but potent attacker.

"Sensors show she's hamstrung that one," said Naquist.

"As you may recall, she performed similar services for us when we were escaping Shortchild, Gemma."

"If we could only have a couple more of those things . . ." Thur said wistfully.

"Mish is working on it. The problem is, we'd need an equal number of blip-ship pilots, and that's part of Laura's magic. It's as though she anticipates each of those shots, knows just when to turn . . . An amazing command of a spacecraft!"

Thur examined a chronometer. "She's got twenty more seconds for us to get a safety margin."

"The way she's going, those cruisers aren't going to be able to follow us anyway!"

They watched the seconds tick past as Laura Shemzak stitched one more path through a spray of rays, then streaked away.

"She made it!" cried Thur.

"Now she's just got to make the short jump here. Damned tricky this close to a gravitational field!" said Naquist.

A wink of light and the blip-ship was gone.

Almost instantaneously it appeared alongside the *Starbow*.

A screech erupted over Tether Mayz's radio controls. "XT, here. I'm comin' in!"

"Docking bay door wide open and shields down, XT," said Tether Mayz. "Welcome."

"And thanks!" Captain Northern called, hands to mouth. "Now then," he said. "Let's see to the business of getting away from this system with our tail still intact!"

Chapter Twenty-one

Each of the Council of Five (minus Overfriend Zarpfrin, currently on field duty) stared blankly at Friend Chivon Lasster.

"This is a most unusual request, Friend Lasster," said Overfriend Visto, a pale thin man nervously puffing a cigarette. His fellows clearly agreed with him, sitting motionlessly around their conference table, computer reference fields humming quietly behind them.

"I thought that Overfriend Zarpfrin," said Chivon, "had mentioned to you that I might be needed to travel in my sector. This business with Tars Northern and the *Starbow* . . . to say nothing of the Jaxdron . . . well, I have submitted my report, gentlefriends. You'll find all the reasons in there."

Overfriend Mazerk, a thick matronly woman with long gray hair, turned her eyes away from the readout hanging in the air behind her, swiveling to face Chivon Lasster. "Yes, this is true. But Lasster, your request is for a personal starship. Now, we realize that you are an excellent pilot. That, after all, is how you were trained. But it is highly irregular for a Friend of your stature to travel without suitable military accompaniment."

"This is simply the way I will feel most comfortable traveling, gentlefriends. My request, I think, states well enough my mission. I only need your approval and cooperation. And as you can see, Overfriend Zarpfrin has already allowed for this possibility."

"Friend Lasster, considering that you merely seek to visit your jurisdiction, albeit for extraordinary purposes—purposes, of course, that have been given our approval," said Overfriend Fernk, with his ever-present doodling pencil momentarily suspended above a piece of paper, "you are well within your area of command. As indicated, we merely are concerned about your desired mode of travel. It is not a safe galaxy anymore, Friend Lasster. You shall need some kind of back-up assistance, I think."

Overfriend Banili lifted a coffee cup to his pinched features and drank. "I agree. Though in respect for Friend Lasster's accomplishments and position, I should like to offer a compromise. A personal starship can certainly be arranged. But perhaps if another trusted member of our Navy can accompany her, we can feel a little more at ease concerning her safety."

Damn, thought Chivon. This will make things much more complicated. Much of the plan she and Andrew had concocted depended upon her being alone in the ship. However, she could not buck any decision that the Council made. At least they agreed she should be allowed to go.

"Yes," said Visto. "That sounds like an excellent idea. Gentlefriends, what say you?"

"I'm still not convinced that this trip is totally necessary," balked Fernk. "After all, Overfriend Zarpfrin is out there right now, and we've received no indication that he needs any assistance in the matter with which he is dealing."

"I believe," responded Chivon, "that I have the capacity to decide when my planets need a visit. Particularly in these trying times," she added firmly.

"Oh, come, come, Fernk, don't be such a spoilsport. If she takes support along with her, there's no reason she can't go," said Overfriend Banili.

The rest agreed.

"Very well, you may leave tomorrow morning at a time to be arranged by this evening," said Overfriend Visto, lighting a new cigarette. "And in the meantime, we will select your company. . . . I can guarantee, Friend Lasster, a suitable enough selection."

Lasster nodded.

Overfriend Fernk gazed over at a list suspended in air.

"First stop on your itinerary is Walthor, I see. Pax Industries and all that. Most fascinating. I belive that you may be able to consult personally with Overfriend Zarpfrin there."

"Yes," said Chivon Lasster. "I very much need to do that."

Chapter Twenty-two

The tail of the *Starbow* remained intact, but not without effort. One of the Federation cruisers still pursued them to the bitter end, when Captain Northern decided they were far enough from the gravitation of the system's sun to penetrate Underspace.

Still, it was a near thing, and a rough ride into Underspace. As usual in such situations, Northern chose to make the jump long before a safety point was reached, and the turbulence and stress on the *Starbow's* frame was considerable, to say nothing about the knocking about the crew received.

But then, that was all a part of the game.

As soon as course was established, Captain Northern announced that a crew meeting would be held after dinner.

Laura Shemzak, cleaned up and feeling good after her little blip-ship exercise, sat down at the table where the military commander robots were serving the meal, and said: "Okay, Northern. Dr. Mish. I don't think I want to wait. I got your asses out of a crack. I want to know now!"

The assembled crew seemed weary from the encounter with the Federation, and not exactly prepared for any space-shaking pronouncements. But Laura was right—her exploits had helped them and their captain, and so the response to Laura's uncouth demand was muted. Besides, some honest curiosity flickered in their aspects.

"Ah, Laura, so glad to see you remaining in character," Captain Northern said. After a soothing shower, he had put on his best uniform. His buttons gleamed in the candlelight, emphasizing the trim cut and excellent material of his outfit. "I had rather hoped that we could eat dinner now, but perhaps my mood is much too formal." His eyes surveyed the group. "Laura refers to my promise to her, or rather, Dr. Mish's promise to her, to explain the whole truth about the nature of the *Starbow*. As you know, part of your duty as members of the crew has been not to ask too many questions. But it has been my observation that we are growing closer, working better together as we strive for our individual and collective goals. We have become as one and it is just as well that certain truths, previously hidden, emerge."

He paused for a moment to let that sink in, then continued. "Our worthy if often rude and troublesome new member, Pilot Laura Shemzak, in a situation which in no way broke her commitment to the *Starbow* and the crew, entered the Hub Room, which as you all know, is off-limits to all. What she discovered there makes it necessary to explain the full story of the *Starbow*." He turned to Laura, sitting beside him. "Please, Laura, tell them what you saw there. Right now you needn't go into how you got there or what happened."

"It was this mammoth monolith—a block," she said, trying to recall the details. "It had this squiggling stuff all around it, like some kind of weird and bizarre alien machine, that was part biological. But one side was like a smooth black mirror. It pulsed with all kinds of strange lights. Damn spooky, I'll tell you!" She leaned over and addressed Dr. Mish. "So, Dr. Mish, what the hell is it? I'm dying to know!"

Dr. Mish smiled pleasantly. "It's really quite simple my dear." He turned his mild gaze to all. "It's a portal."

"A portal?" Laura said. "A portal to where?"

"A portal to Omega Space, a portal to different galaxies, possibly a portal to who knows where else at this time." He took a deep sigh. "But only in potential. Because, you see, it is a very ancient portal, and at the moment it doesn't work at all. I'd very much like to fix it, you see, because it's a part of me."

"Part of you . . . You're the goddamn Guardian that that Jaxdron thing was crowing about!" She looked perplexed. "But why would the Federation build this weird kind of thing?"

"That's just it, Laura. The Federation didn't build it," said Captain Northern. "Ten years ago, in a routine exploratory mission, the Federation ship *Frankfurt* discovered a small flotilla of five alien starships, abandoned for God knows how many millennia in a system at the edge of the known universe. I was on that mission. I helped explore the vessels. The *Starbow*, in a different form, was one of those ships.''

Looks of great surprise appeared on most of the crew's faces.

"And this portal . . . this was on it then? And the other ships . . . did they have portals as well?''

"Oh yes, indeed, but we didn't know what they were. There were so many strange things in the starships. But can you imagine the impact of this discovery upon the Federation authorities?''

"The Overfriends must have wet their drawers!'' Laura said.

"Almost. Imagine. Another race of intelligent creatures with stardrives, operating thousands upon thousands of years ago! What secrets of advanced technology must be hidden on board these spaceships? What knowledge? And best of all, what advanced weaponry! Perhaps, they thought, we can use these ships ourselves!

"But most fascinating of all, when we boarded these ships, they woke up. But they didn't tell us about it. All we knew right away was that we had five usable starships on our hands. Gradually, we came to discover that these starships were actually sentient. But that's a long story and the details on that can wait until some other time. Apparently these entities, including Mish here, were extremely groggy for a long time after we tripped their wake-up call. Groggy and without much memory.''

"Even now,'' Dr. Mish said, toying with his tie, "to this day, I am mostly an amnesiac. But then I am not whole, for my core does not function properly. And what is a Guardian without something to guard?''

"After we became aware of the sentiences and they were deemed harmless,'' Northern continued, "indeed potentially useful, the hull and interiors of the ships were refitted toward a more human-designed look, and the AI project was born, purely to masquerade the true meaning and nature of the project. Overfriend Zarpfrin was placed in command of the ships and I became one of the pilots. Chivon Lasster was my copilot.

"To abbreviate a complicated tale, as the consciousness —friendly and cooperative from the start—began to learn more of their inner natures, they revealed to Zarpfrin their true duties—and the nature of their interiors, the inoperative portals. They requested help in repairing them. I was a part of that campaign.

"But I also was coming to realize that the Overfriends were becoming quite troubled concerning these portals. For you see, as the intelligences remembered back, it was to a universe teeming with strange and exotic civilizations, most warlike, fighting for new territory all the time, here and in other dimensions. Stochastic predictions based on the information presented to us revealed that at least another five hundred years of technological and by-our-bootstraps evolutionary growth is needed by the Federation worlds before it is ready to take its place in the cosmos. In the meantime, Overfriends see humanity—or most importantly, the Federated Empire—as vulnerable to conquest and enslavement by any number of these spacefaring civilizations out there, if they are aware of us.

"Zarpfrin and his fellows saw the portals as a threat. The Federation has no desire for further expansion. It wants to consolidate its gains. If we opened these remarkable mobile portals, God knew what might come crawling through, they thought . . . so they and their alien Guardians were deemed as threats and scheduled for execution.

"I anticipated this move after digging into Overfriend Zarpfrin's private correspondence. I was in a position to do nothing more than 'steal' the *Starbow* and become a free-lancer."

"While I seek quantities of the substance attilium," Dr. Mish said, "which might allow me to reopen my portal . . . and the depths of myself."

"But what about the alien hordes that might come crawling through!" Laura said, alarmed.

"Only the tyrants see other civilizations as threats, Laura. The whole matrix of the universe will be open to us through this wonderful door! How can a free and thinking human being do anything else but feel the need to explore the treasures of this universe and perhaps the next! To seek, to explore, to know the secrets that there are to know! Is this not a wonderful opportunity?"

"And you think, Dr. Mish," said Laura, "that my brother Cal can help you fix this portal."

"Yes, that is most likely."

"But now the Jaxdron know about it, and wouldn't mind having it for their own," Laura said, shaking her head. "As I mentioned, they seemed terribly excited at the prospect."

"Which is why they wouldn't mind trapping us," said Northern. "But that is the chance we'll have to take. Who knows what new talents the doctor and the *Starbow* will own if we can open up the portal and make them whole? I see the whole thing as an answer to our dreams, my crew, my friends. With our knowledge and power, we can serve as a focal point for a coalition of the Free Worlds and thus unite against the threat of the Federation!"

"Just a moment," said Gemma Naquist. "I must admit this explains a lot . . . and I can certainly understand why you haven't told us the whole truth as yet, Tars, though you certainly hinted at this all the time. But exactly what was the purpose of this portal which seems to be the reason for the existence of this ship?"

"Doctor?" said Northern, assigning this task to the robot extension of the *Starbow*.

"I do not fully know yet," Dr. Mish confessed. "As I say, incomplete as I am, most of my memory nodes are either corroded or non-functional. But I have snippets of memories, gleams of dreams . . . inexpressible, all of them. I can only surmise that my creators—the builders of these portals—were somehow overcome by a hostile race. Perhaps they hid the five of us. Perhaps there are more roaming the universe. I strongly suspect that. But there is so much for me to relearn. . . ."

"And by cooperating with our goals, you see the possibility of recovering your memory, your powers," completed Gemma, "and reopening your portal again."

"How do we know that these portals weren't closed for a reason," Laura said. "Like, to keep something out of this universe that ain't supposed to be here."

"Oh, my goodness!" Dr. Mish said, laughing. "You and your brother must have watched a great deal of old movies. Perhaps you even read some H. P. Lovecraft from the sounds of it. Now, do I seem the sinister sort to you?"

"I don't know, Doc, that room you got down there is pretty damned spooky!" said Laura.

"Alien, perhaps, Laura," said Captain Northern. "But certainly no spooks!"

"Sounds like we got a ghost in this machine though," Laura said, jabbing a thumb Dr. Mish's way. "We're not really sure just what you are, are we Doc? I mean, for a while I thought you were human. Then I thought you were an artificial intelligence. Now I find out you're some Guardian. . . ."

"A life form previously unencountered by humanity?" Dr.
Mish said. "I can fully agree that this is the case. As to what
exactly I am . . . well, again, that is a mystery to both me and
you. A mystery which I am hungry to solve." His eyes grew
far off, perhaps even haunted.

Captain Northern took a moment to survey the crew som-
berly. Then he said, "We share this secret with you freely
because we feel this crew has grown into something more than
merely a crew of individuals. But I want you to know that if
any of you, knowing what you know now about our true intents and purposes, feel that you cannot continue with us . . .
or do not wish to participate . . ." He frowned and hung on to
his silence awhile. "Well, we shall be glad to let you off at
some nearby neutral port on our way to our destination." He
smiled just a bit, then swept his gaze slowly from individual to
individual.

Each met him eye to eye.

"Hell, Captain, things were getting boring anyway!" said
one, and laughter volleyed all about.

"One thing I can promise you people," said Captain Northern, pouring himself a glass of wine. "From now on, on the
good ship *Starbow* things will never be dull." He held up the
glass. "To our success on Walthor!"

"To Walthor!" cried the others.

Laura was still bemused at all of this. Ancient alien race . . .
portals . . . a universe teeming with potentially malevolent
civilizations, ready to pounce upon humanity—it all made her
feel very small and insignificant.

But she had to find Cal, no matter what. She had promised
herself that, and if she did nothing else in this life that was
good and true, she kept her word.

A frisson of liveliness swept her that had nothing to do with
the drugs in her body. "You know," she said, grabbing her
own glass and filling it. "Even I'll drink to that!" But she
could take a mere sip. "All right, confession's over. All that
activity has made me damn hungry. Let's eat."

They all supped with excellent appetites.

Chapter
Twenty-three

ATTN: Captain Tars Northern

FROM: Dr. Michael Mish

RE: Walthor/Pax Industries

Captain,

Per your request, I've assembled a brief outline of information concerning our destination, the Federation activities there, and the information accidently culled from Laura Shemzak's memory nodes stocked with leeched information concerning Jaxdron infiltration of Pax Industries.

The planet in Federation Exploratory Charts AB 40 was discovered 153 years ago by a survey expedition mapping the fringes of the nearest Federation-controlled sector (details, type X on your console). Second planet of six orbiting primary Beta Theta; sensor readings indicated it as a perfect world for biotechnological ecoforming into a top secret prison, utilizing prisoners for biotech experiments and as special factory workers for construction of questionable items for various purposes (details, enter 772A into console).

In short, it is a place few members of either the Federation or the Free Worlds know about, yet it serves as a detention place for criminals, a laboratory world, and a manufacturing world for specialized products.

Walthor itself, with an 86 degree axial tilt and a regular orbit, combined with a high water-land ratio, is a planet lush with flora and fauna and natural resources. Three separate species of intelligent alien life—all agricultural/hunters, all pre-industrial—have been subjugated in various ways by the Federation for use in exploiting the planet. None of this has been through military means, though a military security force is stationed on the planet, but rather by the anthropological/cultural brainwashing that has been so successful not only on many other planets, but on the Federation's people themselves. (For further information on separate species, type 542B on your console.)

The planet's computer network and central operational building lies within what is simply known as the Block. It was here that Laura Shemzak was sent to test the strong security measures against outside infiltration. Her mission was successful and she tapped into the Heart Computer, stealing a large amount of information. Immediately following this effort, she learned of the capture of her brother by the Jaxdron, and shipped back to Earth. Apparently in the confusion, her superiors neglected to debrief her properly and wipe away this recording she had taken in breaching the Block's security.

During the removal of the implant which forced her to shoot her brother, this memory node was tapped into. Analysis indicates direct reference to Jaxdron infiltration of Pax Industries—and possible manufacture of devices shipped throughout the human universe for purposes of subjugation and conquest. It is possible that through these means, the Jaxdron discovered not only the nature of the work being performed upon Mulliphen, but the nature of Cal Shemzak's activities, and thus thought to kidnap him for their own purposes.

However, the actual details included in the leeched material were scanty.

• • •

In working out the possibilities, I am convinced that rather than pursue the Jaxdron blindly to a place they apparently want us to be (most likely a trap), further information might be obtained by having Laura Shemzak once more infiltrate the Heart Computer and determine exactly the nature of Jaxdron activity there.

As to how this will be done, that would be left up to Laura Shemzak, since she has the full knowledge of and contacts on the planet.

They landed just outside a small alien village in a clearing of the jungle by the side of a river.

Laura was sweating from the exertion and concentration of dealing with the extra weight. The compartment in the rear of the vessel was designed for supplies and souvenirs, not a full-grown human being.

Her consciousness folded back in on itself slowly as she began to disengage herself from her interface with the blip-ship, satisfied that the vessel was on solid ground and wouldn't sink into quicksand or slide into the river.

"Can I get out now?" said Captain Tars Northern, his voice muffled within the compartment. "I feel like I've been buried alive!"

"Told you it wouldn't be long, though, didn't I?" said Laura, fighting the disorientation that always came when she changed from blip-ship consciousness to normal human consciousness. "Besides, you were the one who wanted to come along! Let me tell you, your extra weight was a true headache!" Laura leaned over behind her and released the catch. The hatch sprang open, revealing Captain Tars Northern securely harnessed into a horizontal squat.

"Any length of time is too long for a claustrophobe!" growled Northern.

"You didn't tell me you were a claustrophobe, Northern!" Laura said as she pushed the buttons that released the harnesses.

"I think I am now!" he said and grinned, getting out of the cramped space.

"Phony phobia if I ever heard of one," Laura shot back. "You just like to complain."

Northern would have followed her down to the surface

of Walthor but for one problem: the intense security measures that surrounded this world. Patrolling ships, radar—you name it and this place had it. A shuttle would have set off all the alarms, but Laura's XT Mark Nine was specially fitted with a cloaking device able to easily hide its activities. Besides, after spending over a month here on her Federation mission, she knew the systems of Pax Industries very well. If anyone could penetrate this planet's security measures—again—it was Laura Shemzak.

The problem, as Laura readily pointed out, was that as good as the blip-ship was, it could not remain undetected if it landed on the Block or its nearby spaceport. Some other route had to be taken.

"You're sure we're in the right place?" Tars Northern said, looking doubtfully around at the cornucopia of foliage as Laura secured the hatch on the XT. "Looks like a three-dee set for one of those old Tarzan pictures."

"Oh, yes, this is the place all right. I know you couldn't see it with your limited view, but we passed over the M'towi village I mentioned. I've got a pretty good memory of that village, believe you me!"

"Right then," said Northern. "If you say so, I believe you."

He wasn't kidding. A trust had grown in Northern for Laura's word, and it touched her deeply. She felt a sudden impulse to kiss him, but uncharacteristically, she held back.

No, she thought. You can't let this guy have a centimeter that way. His roguishness was charming, his trust ingratiating, but a gal could definitely get in trouble falling prey to the physical expression of any kind of affection with this cad. Still . . .

"Glad to hear that, Northern. Got your equipment and your gun? Good, 'cause you're going to need it."

Under the hot sun there was already a trace of perspiration growing on Northern's brow.

"Oh. Did you bring your deodorant? You're going to need that too."

"Umm . . . well, actually . . . might I borrow yours?"

"Automatic, my friend. Cyborg attachment. You spend weeks cooped up in that little ship, you've gotta have some arrangement."

"How peculiar," said Tars Northern. "Well then, you'll have to excuse me."

"I'll just stay upwind, okay?" She winked at him. "C'mon, let's get going. If we're lucky, we'll catch a couple of my pals on siesta."

"Seems like a good thing to be doing about this time," Northern said. "I wonder if they're sipping nice cool drinks. Compatible metabolisms, Laura?"

"Oh yes. They're the most humanoid of the three sorts of intelligent life on this planet. So compatible, in fact, that at first they developed a taste for human flesh. The Federation cured them of that soon enough."

"What a pleasant bit of news, Laura," Northern said.

"I thought you should be fully informed."

They struck off through the jungle, following a trail Laura vaguely remembered from her last circumspect visit. True, she had not smuggled herself in quite in this manner: she had presented herself as a skilled technician from the planet Romulos who had been hired for basic peripheral computer work in the field. From this base she had to learn about the Block and what techniques she needed to infiltrate its core, testing its security provisions. But in her work with the myriad extensions of the controlling computer, she had done some field work, encountering this particular M'towi tribe only kilometers away from the Block when their communications computer went down. She spent a whole day there, troubleshooting the system quickly but stalling long enough to get to know the people of the tribe.

"They really are quite interesting. I visited them once again before I got into the core, just to say hello," Laura said as they bashed their way through a troublesome collection of frondlike vegetation overhanging the trail.

"And so that's why we're here now?" said Northern in a griping tone. "To pay a hello call to a bunch of your alien pals?" Already, perspiration was streaming down his face.

"No, stupid," said Laura. "I told you, this will be the fastest and easiest way to sneak into the compound."

"I took your word for it then, but I didn't know we'd be traveling through a steam bath!"

"It will sweat some of that junk you drink out of your system, Northern. Get you in shape!"

"I'll have you know I work out, I stay in shape—it's just damned hot and sticky here," Northern replied, trudging gamely after her. "So tell me this plan again. Mish gave it his okay but I was too busy to go over it."

"Blind trust, eh?" Laura remarked snappily, but inside she was touched that Captain Northern had developed this much faith in her.

"Hardly blind, Laura. You're one of the best operatives I've ever seen. A simple, empirically proven fact."

Her eyes shone as she stopped a moment and looked back at him. "Thank you, Captain. Now this is very simple. This M'towi tribe regularly visits the Block compound to deliver various fruits and vegetables and other supplies they sell to the people there, in addition to the normal work they're assigned. It happens that I dealt with the M'towi in charge of this daily delivery, and I'm sure I'll be able to revive our friendship. Believe me, he has no love for the Federation. He was one of the rebels who was put down years ago."

"Ah yes—very good. But exactly what are the details of this infiltration?"

She halted in a muddy patch, reached back, and tweaked his nose. "Just you wait and see!"

Tars Northern spoke as though he expected the native village to be a collection of grass huts complete with boiling pots and tribal dancers. When the trail opened up into a clearing containing something entirely different, he could not hide his surprise.

Amidst the greenish sun's pounding heat stood a cluster of multilevel structures of subtle architectural design. Beyond, stretched a few fields of indeterminate nature. A group of dark-skinned humanoid aliens wearing white pantaloons and wide-brimmed hats stood on the steps to a building, talking to each other in a strange language containing numerous clicks and hums.

"Do they speak Standard Galactic?" Northern asked doubtfully.

"A few words."

"But how are you going to speak to them?"

"You forget that I am a highly resourceful ex-secret agent of the Federated Empire, Tars Northern." She pulled up the left sleeve of her shirt and completed a series of coded pressure points. "You also forget my cyborg components." A length of synthetic skin rolled back and she dialed in a number on a control face. "There. I can now approximate the M'towi speech. How do you think I communicated with them in the first place?"

"My amazement is unbounded, O mistress of the starways." Northern beckoned her politely to proceed with her intentions.

"Stay here a moment, out of sight," she said, then struck off toward the talking natives. None of them was her friend Xersi, so she hoped they might tell her where he could be found.

The aliens stiffened at the sight of the human in their midst. "Who are you?" asked one, his double proboscis twitching—a sign of nervousness amongst the M'towi. "We are not scheduled for a Federation meeting this day!"

Laura opened her mouth and her mechanical implementation immediately cut in to her speech center, allowing her to speak their tongue. "Hello. Perhaps you remember me. I was here last season. I seek Xersi, whom I dealt with before."

The aliens murmured amongst themselves, their long, delicate fingers moving languidly, like seaweed in a slow current, their eyes darting back to Laura suspiciously.

"Do not be concerned," said Laura holding her hand up in a M'towi sign of loyalty to tribe and conspiracy. They blinked with surprise that she knew this gesture. "Xersi and I have shared gloc tea and have sung to the sun in harmony. We both are not friends to the Block."

The aliens nodded their heads—not a native gesture, but an affectation they'd learned from human beings. "In that case, there is no harm," one of them said. "Come with us and we will bring you to his gloc time. He's due to emerge from trance soon."

"One moment. I have brought a companion with me. We both must speak to Xersi."

The aliens shrugged and one spoke in Standard Galactic. "What the hell. The more the merrier!"

The room had a dirt floor and was filled with shadows shifting with the flickers of three candle flames placed in corners of the room. It smelled of subterranean musk, and being dug into the ground, was much cooler than outside. A hint of aromatic

incense laced the air. Laura recognized the smell of the ceremonial gluc tea in the air and immediately hoped Xersi would
offer them some. That stuff packed a buzz!

The alien ushered them in politely, and Northern looked
around with his usual suspicion and cynicism. "Looks like
your kind of place, Laura. Where's your pal?"

"Shush!" Laura commanded, finger to lips. "Have some
couth, fellow! This is a time of individual meditation for the
M'towi and it deserves respect."

"Couth?" Northern returned tartly. "You're asking me for
couth?" But he'd lowered his voice to a bare whisper.

The M'towi who had led them inside gestured them to halt.
"I go wake up the gluc head now. He has been here too long
anyway! He is such a glutton with the tea!"

"What did he say?" asked Northern.

"He wants to know if we can use the handsome starship
captain for a sacrifice. The gods are hungry this day. I'll tell
him I hope they like their food well lubricated."

Northern let that pass.

The M'towi ambled over to a figure that sat far back in the
room, huddling amidst the shadows.

"Northern, I want you to notice the solemnity and dignity
of the ritual awakening," said Laura.

As their eyes grew accustomed to the dimness, they could
see that the figure was curled up into a kind of lumpy fetal ball
with appendages, atop a large square blanket of complex
designs. Before him was a large wooden bowl filled almost to
the brim with a dark frothy liquid. The squatting figure's long
fingers still clutched what appeared to be a stone cup.

The approaching alien stopped just in front of Xersi, then
suddenly kicked him over. "Wake up, you lazy blank brain!"

The squatting alien scrambled up to his feet, weaving in the
dark dizzily. "I thank you, brother, for pulling me out of my
ecstasy. Is it your turn now?"

"No. You have visitors. One of them claims to be your
friend of last season. They wish to speak to you."

"I am moved," said Northern. "Truly moved."

The M'towi motioned them over, then lit another set of
candles. The alien called Xersi stared for a moment with his
limpid eyes, then cried out, "But of course! It is the computer
repair lady! Welcome back, Marilyn Monroe!"

"Marilyn Monroe?" Northern asked, for Xersi had spoken in broken Standard Galactic.

Laura was glad of the dimness; it hid her blush. "Uh . . . yeah, that was my alias for my Intelligence job here." She was too embarrassed to ask if he knew who Marilyn Monroe had been on old Earth. "Let's not confuse him though, okay?"

"Anything you say, Marilyn," returned Northern with a broad smile, glad of ammunition for future verbal ripostes.

Laura turned back to Xersi and spoke to him in his own language. "Yes, my friend, I have returned from the stars. I have traveled far distances since last we met. Might we sit down? Our human legs are much inferior to the mighty thews of the M'towi, and we are tired."

"Ah, such glib garbage all you Terraspawn speak on first greeting," said Xersi. "I remember one of the first diplomats you sent to cheat us years back. Longtongue, we came to call him. But sit, sit, for I have thought of you much since your departure, female Terraspawn."

They sat down on the rough-textured blanket. Xersi requested the other to bring back a glass of water. "You may take some of the gloc in water and it is not so powerful and it is very refreshing. Now what have you come about, friend Marilyn?"

"You remember, do you not Xersi, when we drank gloc together undiluted and we shared secrets of our hearts?" Laura said as softly and urgently as she could in such a rough language.

"Aye, I remember very well. You touched me by sharing my hatred for those who control us all. And you told me of a sibling who you cared for very much."

"Yes. My brother, Cal."

The other native returned with glasses of cool water. Xersi dipped his stone cup into the bowl of gloc and offered to drip some into their glasses.

"Just what is that stuff?" Northern asked doubtfully.

"Take my word, you'll like it, Captain."

The dark stuff dyed the water a muddy brown. Laura took a sip. It was sweet and bitter and good. The heat of the day and the strain in her muscles was immediately forgotten.

"Ah, thank you, Xersi," she said. "The deep roots of the yunga tree are yet true." She put the glass down.

"Not bad, thank you," said Northern.

"Yes," said Laura. "Cal. My brother. In a very real way, that is why I have returned, Xersi. I do not know if you are aware of this, but my people now fight a very huge war with creatures called the Jaxdron. My brother is a brilliant person and the Jaxdron feel that they can use him, so they have stolen him. I seek to get him back, and that is why I am here."

"Ah yes! We have heard of the Jaxdron!" said Xersi. "But they are not here! You have come to the wrong place!"

"Let me explain. I no longer work for the Friends, Xersi. I am a renegade. They were using me, and I rebelled. They tried to use me to kill my brother when I found him. This man helped me find my brother, and he is my friend now. He is a Star Hound, Xersi."

"Ah, excellent. Perhaps we can hire his fleet to liberate my people from the Federation!"

"I'm afraid he has only one starship, though he is definitely working against the Federation, and you can fight the Federation by aiding us!"

"Tell me what I must do!" said the M'towi eagerly.

"It's really very simple, my friend. Since the Federation is now my enemy, I cannot enter the Block. And in order to fight the Federation and save my brother, Captain Northern and I must enter the Block for a short period of time and then exit without Governor Bartlick or his men knowing. Are you still making regular deliveries to the Block, Xersi?"

"I am indeed! And tomorrow morning at dawn I make my next." Suddenly, his eyes brightened. "Ah ha! And you wish me help smuggle you in!"

"You're a pretty smart guy for a gloc head, Xersi."

"Hey," said Northern. "This stuff is pretty good!" He held out his empty glass. "Can I have some more?"

Chapter Twenty-four

They were shown to their room after the evening meal. It was a simple affair, with human-type beds, used to house guests from the Block's compound.

"I shall come for you to prepare you an hour before dawn. You will be ready then, yes?" Xersi said.

Captain Northern collapsed onto one of the beds.

"Oh yes, yes," said Laura. "Thank you, Xersi."

The alien fluttered his fingers, indicating both Laura and Tars Northern. "You two . . . You are a human sex-bound couple? Don't make too much noise, please, you'll scare the children!"

"We are no such thing!" Laura cried, outraged.

"Just be quiet when you mate, please," said the native closing the door behind him.

Laura went over to the window, shaking her head wearily. Her brain still seemed a bit off kilter, what with the gloc she had taken, though she was clearly not as messed up as Northern. Strange, he seemed to almost live on alcohol and stayed coherent and sharp, if a touch wild. Laura never touched the stuff. It seemed to interfere with the operation of her cyborg systems and made her sick besides. But gloc and its chemical sisters and brothers with psychoactive properties gave her a glow of good feeling and nothing more.

Apparently, it knocked Northern head over heels. He was sprawled out on the bed, arms akimbo, eyes closed. She went

over to tuck him in. Wouldn't do to have a starship captain
with a cold.

At the touch of her hand, he reached out for her. She almost
shoved him away, but his touch was so gentle, his attentions so
weak, she knew she could separate herself at anytime with a
minimum of fuss.

She might just be able to get something out of him in this
state, she thought. Besides, it didn't feel bad at all. . . .

"Mmm," he said languidly, wrapping his arms around her
waist. "Laura, darling, you are such a tart delight."

"You had too much gloc, Tars," she said, settling against
him tentatively, enjoying his warmth and the hard comfort of
his powerful body but trying not to let herself relax. She
sensed the danger of any kind of surrender to him; an emotional pitfall that must be avoided. "Don't worry. It's really
marvelously free of aftereffects."

It was for her, anyway. She hoped it had the same effect on
Tars. Which reminded her . . .

"Tars, why do you drink so much?"

"Thirsty!" he said drowsily, tracing imaginary pictures
delicately across her back with his fingertips.

"No, its something more than that, Tars. You drink like an
alcoholic and yet you can get cleaned of that very quickly.
Mish monitors your consumption. What gives?"

"I like it!" he murmured drowsily. "Now give us a kiss!"

She took a different tack. "What do you want from me,
starship Captain? Really."

"Your delicious affections, my dear. Now why are we wast-
ing time!" But he said it all without conviction, as though
from rote. Perhaps he meant it, but the gloc rendered his
words spineless.

"I'd just be using you, Tars," she said condescendingly.
"But I am interested in why you drink alcohol."

Northern shrugged. "I'm not real sure. I always drank.
Then, when I got the *Starbow* one evening, alone with a bottle
of wine . . . I felt something deeper in me, something added.
That's the evening I got to know Mish better. I became more
than I really seemed to be. I dunno, like the well of my unconscious just got deeper and richer in content. And from then on
I could grasp what Mish was talking about."

Laura blinked, surprised. An interesting notion.

"You mean the alcohol changes your brain chemistry so that some kind of subliminal telepathic link forms with your ship?"

"I dunno. Something like that. Have to ask Mish for the exact details. But that was one of the reasons he was able to convince me of the nature of his being . . . and its essential rightness." His words, despite their dullness, seemed heartfelt. "Not good stuff, alcohol. I hate it sometimes. But it's necessary . . . and Mish makes sure . . . minimum of toxin . . . damage."

He was fading fast.

"God's own drunk," murmured Laura. She tapped him lightly on the cheek to keep him barely conscious.

"Hmm?" said Northern. "What . . . ?"

"Why so many women, Tars Northern? I suppose you're going to tell me that *they* open up a link between you and the cosmos."

"I can't keep 'em away," Northern said, a fat smile suddenly crossing his face. "I'm such a good lover!"

"Sure."

"Try me sometime, Pilot!"

"It's more than that, isn't it?"

"Maybe. You kind of like me, don't you?"

"Bullshit. I think you're an arrogant, complicated buffoon who happens to play into my needs. I'm using you, baby, and don't you forget it."

"Use me anytime, sweetheart."

"You should be so lucky!" she harrumphed, and quickly stood up and moved away from him.

"Sorry," he said, eyes still closed. "Long as I'm telling the truth, might as well say I do find you . . . different, Laura Shemzak. Perhaps Fate is playing with us. Perhaps we're just too good for one another."

"Bullshit," she said.

He started snoring lightly.

She watched him awhile then put a blanket over him and sat down beside him, resting her hand gently on his leg.

He was handsome, even in sleep. A much more innocent handsomeness at that, without those deep knowing eyes mocking and flickering and teasing.

Suddenly, she was quite glad that he'd come along. Not

only for the help on this mission—help she was too proud to admit she needed—but for their talk and for this time together.

She looked at him again, and noticed her feelings flowing. Instantly, she staunched them, removed her hand, stood up and walked away.

Suddenly, she felt sick to her stomach. The universe was suddenly so cold, so very cold and scary . . . and if she slipped up, if she made the slightest mistake in certain areas, it would rear up and smash her like an annoying fly.

Damn! What was wrong with her? This wasn't the Laura Shemzak who stared the stars straight in the eye and spit. This wasn't the Laura Shemzak who'd turned the Federation on its ear to save her brother.

No, this was a different Laura, she realized. A Laura who was just as frightened as any other human being. Frightened about tomorrow, when she would face the might of the Federation she had betrayed? No. She was frightened of . . . of something else.

Laura thought to check her dosage of blip drug, but she stopped herself. No, that wasn't the problem at all.

She turned off the light without looking at Tars Northern, got into her bed, and pulled up the covers until she was warm and cozy.

But she knew she wasn't safe. She took a deep breath and shuddered because she knew she was in terrible danger.

Her only comfort was the obnoxiousness of the turkey's snores.

Chapter Twenty-five

When the shuttle landed late at night at Walthor Starport, Friend Chivon Lasster waited for it on the tarmac. Her own starship, the *Eagle*, was berthed not far away, silvery tip pointed toward the glittery canopy of stars. The ensign the Council had sent with her had already turned in for the night.

The ramp slid out, touching the ground emphatically. In only a few moments Friend Zarpfrin was pounding down it, as though in a hurry.

"Welcome to Walthor," said Lasster, smiling wryly.

Zarpfrin did a double take. "Friend Lasster . . . what are you doing here?"

"I thought it necessary to help you oversee operations. Aren't you pleased to see me?"

Zarpfrin gestured brusquely for her to accompany him and his entourage. "It's just as well. Things have heated up a bit."

"The war. . . . ?"

"No . . . this Northern business."

She tried to control her emotions from rising to her voice. "Oh?"

"Yes. But it's muggy out here, and I'm hungry. Let's go and have a late dinner and I'll tell you all about it."

Zarpfrin pushed back his plate and patted his protuberant stomach in a satisfied manner.

Chivon Lasster was still astonished. "You almost had him," she said.

"Yes," said Zarpfrin. "Right in my lap! If I had been prepared . . . well, we would have had the bastard and his ship. You would have liked that, wouldn't you?"

She nodded. "Yes. Yes, I suppose I would."

"Well, no matter. I settled things with Freeman Jonst. Ruffled feathers all around, but the plan is still working."

"As it is everywhere."

"Yes." Zarpfrin sipped his coffee. "And why shouldn't it? Those colonies are scared. Naturally they should accept the help of their fellow humans. We have made the very best of a bad situation, Friend Lasster, have we not? And as the architect of the plan, how can I not take satisfaction in its obvious efficiency?"

"Let's just hope the Jaxdron are truly repelled if they do choose to attack these Free Worlds the Federation is protecting."

"Oh, I suspect we may well lose a few. But think of all the ones we will gain. Back in the Federation, Lasster. Once the aliens are repelled, we will have total power over these planets. A little gunboat diplomacy, some institutional and social manipulation, and within fifteen years they will be full members once more of the Human Federation. With outposts in the very center of the Free Worlds, we can begin working on the other worlds. Within a generation, now that travel and communications have been speeded up tremendously, humankind will exist in solidarity. My dream, Lasster . . . this is what my life is dedicated to!"

"Yes, and I have been of some help, have I not, Zarpfrin?"

"Oh, yes, indeed you have, my dear. Without your administration abilities, the organization of this project would not have been possible. Without a doubt, you will be rewarded, Friend Lasster. All our ambitions will be rewarded handsomely, I'm sure."

"It is too bad you lost Tars Northern, though," said Lasster.

"Oh," Zarpfrin said, his eyes twinkling. "I think we might have another chance sometime soon with him. But how go our operations on Walthor? I presume that this is the reason for your visit here."

"Yes. Production on the devices is being kept up. Within

two years, at my estimate, dissemination throughout the empire and most of the Free Worlds will be complete, and we shall be able to have reconnaissance of every world with our spy devices. Already, the computers are working at full efficiency, compiling signals into a comprehensive overview of the situation everywhere."

"Excellent! Your contribution is most appreciated, Friend Lasster."

Her contributions, thought Chivon Lasster. Yes, she had made many contributions. She had been devoted to this task that Zarpfrin had spoken of . . . for years now. To reunite the Federation—it seemed so grand an idea, so important. Together with Arnal Zarpfrin, she had set this scheme in motion, this brilliant opportunity that had fallen into their laps with the advent of the war with the Jaxdron.

So simple, so beautiful . . . it could not fail. But now, with what she knew, she knew it had to fail.

"One matter, though, Zarpfrin, I should like to bring up." Lasster paused, choosing her words carefully.

"And what is that, Friend Lasster?" Zarpfrin said, placing his cup back in its saucer and lacing his fingers together, fixing his attention fully upon his underling.

"I wonder if your fixation with Tars Northern might not be draining needed attention from other aspects of your projects. I wonder, Friend Zarpfrin, if I might be allowed to assume full responsibility for his search."

Zarpfrin blinked. "I know well your feelings on the matter of Northern, but I wonder why you request this, Lasster."

"To relieve you of the effort, as I said."

"I don't think that will be necessary, Friend Lasster. As I hinted, I have the matter well in hand."

"But surely you realize that if your plan with Laura Shemzak worked, then she will join forces with him and most certainly come looking for you. I mean causing her to kill that brother of hers is deadly stuff."

"I have taken that into account. And you are quite right. Laura Shemzak's XT Mark Nine was used successfully in escaping Federation forces. She is quite alive and no doubt would very much like to deal with me in a harsh and nasty fashion. But I have, as I mentioned, allowed for all that and am quite prepared for that eventuality."

"Ah, I see. But there's more to this AI business than you're letting on, isn't there? You need the *Starbow* . . . that's why you're so desperate to get it.''

"It works against the Federation now, it works against me—of course I should very much like to either capture it or destroy it. But to reiterate, I can very well handle the situation.'' He smiled mischievously. "In fact, it may very well be the case, Friend Lasster, that the matter may be dealt with very soon. Now, I should retire. I trust that you'll take me for a tour of facilities in the morning?''

Lasster nodded, wondering what Zarpfrin was talking about but not willing to press the subject.

Chapter Twenty-six

The first rays of the alien sun over the jungles of Walthor found a caravan of trucks moving onto the paved road that led to the Block compound. In the front of one of the trucks sat three beings: one driver and two passengers. Uncomfortable passengers.

"Haven't they got any air-conditioning in this heap?" asked Tars Northern. "This outfit is killing me."

"You'll just have to endure it, Tars," said Laura Shemzak. "Air-conditioning awaits us, I assure you."

They both wore extremely detailed latex masks which made them look like M-towi tribesmen, along with the ceremonial robes of Walthor traders. Beside them, Xersi drove silently and intently, concentrating on keeping the truck dead center on the narrow road.

"For once, I'm actually looking forward to putting myself into the clutches of the Federation. At least it will be cool there."

"Other than sweaty, how are you?"

"Just fine, thank you." He turned toward her, though she could not read his expression through the mask. "Relaxed, actually, Laura. You were right about the gluc . . . no after-effects. Though I can't remember exactly what happened last night."

"Nothing. We went back after our talk with Xersi and you collapsed."

"My rotten luck. Alone with a beautiful and passionate woman, and I had to be crocked."

"Wouldn't have done you any good if you'd been totally straight, Tars, I quite assure you."

She paused, wondering whether or not to tell him. Why not? she thought. "I did pry some interesting things out of you, though."

"Did you now?" Tars' eyes kept straight ahead, staring at the passing viny treetops, voice suddenly emotionless.

"Nothing to worry about. Just a deep secret."

"Oh?"

"I asked why you drank so much, and you told me the truth. I'd wondered why you seemed so close to Dr. Mish—I mean, the ship—and now I know. It's that simple."

"Ah . . . yes."

"Which explains why you didn't bring a flask or anything. You're out of range of subliminal contact with Mish, so you don't need to drink alcohol."

"Doesn't mean I wouldn't take a martini with lunch, Laura," said Northern. "Truth to tell, doesn't mean I wouldn't take a cold gin fizz right now. Though a glass of water would do, I suppose."

Laura asked Xersi for a canteen and they drank.

"You're sure this is going to work?" Northern said.

"Xersi says that the guards barely notice the help. We'll get in, and while we're helping to unload the trucks, we can just take off."

"Lucky you know the Block's compound."

"Yes, it is fortunate." She looked out of the front window. Rising up from the tops of the trees in the distance, the high-rises of the compound grew like sculpted mountains. "There they are, Northern. Let's get this straight. I slip off and repeat my computer leech number while you skulk about the manufacturing area, checking for Jaxdron spy devices."

"But not in this get-up, fortunately." Xersi had provided them both with Federation uniforms so they could blend in. "I'm not real crazy being an alien."

"Hey, just remember, on this planet you're the alien."

"Right." He glanced over at the M'towi, still intently driving. "You've thanked him for his help?"

"Oh yes. And he's more than happy to work against the

Federation in any way he can.''

Xersi seemed to sense the tack the conversation had taken. "If there is anything else that I may do . . .''

"No, Xersi," said Laura, reverting to the native's language. "You're taking enough risk as it is.''

The being's skin seemed somehow paler in this early morning light, though Laura had no way of knowing what emotions were being reflected in its face. Even though she was capable of understanding and speaking the language with the help of her implanted device and had spent time with them before, she actually knew very little about the deeper motivations within the native Walthorian peoples.

"Very well," said Xersi. "As you wish. Unloading and business matters and such can be stretched out to a maximum of three hours. The compound will harbor unadapted Walthor life no longer than that.''

Laura translated for Northern, who agreed they could easily accomplish their mission in that time period.

"Unadapted?" Northern asked. "What does he mean by that?''

"Biological slaves concocted by the Federation using the three native intelligent species, with a few other interesting native species thrown in for good measure. They call them Conglomerates, and they wear identity meshes wired to their nervous systems. Sort of like biological robots—needless to say, it's one of the Federation's crimes here on this distant outpost. We might well find evidence to support the fact that the Feddies are looking to spread these kind of factory worlds, and experiments with Conglomerates, to other worlds. That, Captain Northern, will go a long way toward convincing the Free Worlds to stay free, and toward organizing them into a group effort to stay so!''

Northern tapped his pocket. "Well, I've got my camera, so—''

"You really needn't have bothered," said Laura, tapping her left eye. "Every biologically implanted Feddy agent has plenty of interior paraphernalia.''

"You just worry about doing the necessary computer taps, Laura Shemzak," Northern said. "That's the most important thing, not snapping tourist pictures.''

"Yes, O lord and master!''

"Oh, and you might start working up a speech on Federation atrocities. You may be right, it could be a valuable political tool."

Laura smiled at his approval, despite herself. "Yes, Captain, I certainly will. You must give me a few pointers of speech making, though. You seem to enjoy that part of your captaincy the most."

"Only too glad to help out, my dear," he replied in a mock-condescending manner.

The convoy consisted of four large trucks. They were the third in line. The trucks stopped in front of the walled gate to the compound, the initial identification screenings were made by human guards, and one by one the trucks rumbled through the passage. As predicted by Xersi, identification was not checked on passenger-helpers along for the ride.

Their truck rolled through the gate, traveled some distance beside a huge building, then turned down a ramp and into a tunnel that led to the bowels of the building. Within a minute the tunnel opened into a huge subterranean chamber. A number of unloading bays lined one wall.

"This is it," Xersi told Laura as he wheeled his truck around, to back it as near as possible to the dock. "Over there are the doors I told you about. No security. The rest is as I described it to you . . . and as you remember. It's up to you. Just be back within the time I've allowed."

They hopped out and went to work, helping to unload the contents of the truck—mostly produce. After a few minutes work, when they were reasonably sure they were not being watched, Northern and Laura ducked into the shadows of the hold and removed their disguises, emerging dressed in the khaki coveralls emblazoned with the standard emblem of the human worker in the compound: a seven-pointed star.

They traveled past the conveyer belts where the produce was being loaded, and entered the hallway where they would split up.

Laura nodded at Northern, he winked at her, then they went their separate ways wordlessly, knowing full well the dangers they could be walking into.

Laura was particularly worried about Northern—after all, he usually functioned as head of a team, and now he was on his own. And while she had the plans of the compound mnemonically emblazoned within, as well as experience with these hallways, Northern only had a rough idea and a mental ball of thread to find his way back.

Still, she thought as she made her way through the long passageway, he doesn't seem daunted in the least, and he has years of experience with this sort of rough and tumble pi-merc stuff. I shouldn't worry.

But nonetheless, she did.

Chapter
Twenty-seven

As Tars Northern walked through the hallways of the Block compound as unobtrusively as possible, he wondered, not for the first time that day, why he had come here to Walthor with Laura Shemzak.

All the other crew members had discouraged him. After all, Laura Shemzak with all her abilities, should have been able to determine the nature and specifics of the Jaxdron infiltration of Pax Industries as a solo agent. Yet the day before the mission, as he had sat in communion with a bottle of Freeman Jonst's brandy and Dr. Mish, they had both decided he should go.

"A hunch?" said Mish.

"Yes. And don't deny that you feel it too, damn you, Mish. There's something else that needs to be taken care of down on the planet. I can't put my finger on it, but it's there."

"Yes, yes, I agree," Mish responded, "but as you well know, I should not like to lose you, Tars Northern. You are much too important to all of us and there is great threat on Walthor. When I put forward the notion of stopping on Walthor to determine the nature of Jaxdron activity there, I did not intend for you to volunteer to land there yourself."

"But you know I must."

"Yes, I know that. I have accustomed myself to your *musts*, Tars Northern. At least they keep things exciting. But tell me, I sense that you also *must* go because of the girl."

"Nonsense!"

"Do not dissemble with me, my companion. I know you too well. You care for her more than you'd like to admit."

"Well, sure I'd like to get in her pants!" Northern had agreed. "I'm as randy as the next egomaniacal starship captain. But care for her? She's got the class of a storm trooper and the manners of an army boot! I'm going along because . . . because this is too vital a mission to leave solely in her wire-ridden hands!"

Mish smiled. "Say what you wish, Northern, but you know what you say is not entirely true. Somehow the girl has begun to touch you in ways you will not admit."

As he passed through a doorway into an area denser with humans, he concentrated more on his task and less on idle speculation. Yes, he had to admit, he was rather fond of Laura Shemzak. Who wouldn't be? She was quite pretty and quite a character, and she aroused him. But romantic feelings? No. In this case, the wise doctor was dead wrong.

Tars Northern stepped onto a slidewalk, keeping alert for his destination: the experimental laboratories. When Laura Shemzak had told him about their existence, he knew that this was something that could be used against the Federation.

Apparently, this remote world served a multiplicity of purposes, one of which was as a prison world for the Federation. Prisoners were being biologically tampered with. The natives of Walthor were being used in this manner as well. Proof of these horrors, as yet unknown to any of the Free Worlds, would certainly make those planets' governments think twice about any unholy alliance with the Federated Empire!

Automatically as he thought about the subject, Tars Northern tapped his shirt, feeling the outlines of both his camera and his small weapon—a needler. He hoped he only needed to use the former.

So far so good, he thought as the slidewalk whisked him on his way past the signs Laura had told him to expect. And the uniform was good too. He aroused no suspicion from the various Federation employees he passed.

It took four minutes to get to the area marked LAB. Northern chuckled to himself as he stepped off the walk. The Feddies were certainly confident enough of themselves and their employees, clearly marking an area where terrible experiments were taking place. But then, Tars Northern remembered the things he had done as a Feddy. He had been so indoctrinated then, so inured . . .

That's what happened to the human spirit in the hands of the kind of social and cultural programming the Federation used to control its peoples. It became warped, unbalanced. He would be forever grateful to the entity he called Dr. Mish for knocking him loose of his particular mental chains.

There was a bank of doors before him, and Northern didn't know which one to enter. Randomly, he chose the leftmost door and pushed his way in to what appeared to be a lobby. There was a desk in the reception area, but no guard manned it.

Funny, thought Northern. You'd think they'd have some kind of security for a project of this nature. Maybe the guard had just stepped out for a cup of coffee.

Northern stepped through the next door and found himself in a long, poorly lit corridor. Various humans were walking through the hallway in pairs and singly, most wearing lab smocks but some dressed just as he was dressed.

Good, thought Northern, stalking forward, not knowing where he was going but following his instincts. I blend in somewhat.

He walked a ways down the hall. Then, randomly again, he chose a door and opened it. It proved to be a closet. So much for my instincts, he thought.

The next one, however, was faintly lit with reddish glow by strips along the side. In the distance, Northern could hear the faint sounds of humming and bubbling. Laboratory sounds, certainly! He ventured forward.

The passageway widened, leading to another door, which opened onto a steel catwalk overlooking a huge hall. Below were a number of large tubs and tables, ranked in rows, over which doctors and technicians worked.

This was it!

Quickly, Northern knelt down and pulled his tiny camera out. Apparently, no one noticed his presence, which meant he had time. The instrument automatically focused as he put the viewfinder to his eye, directed it at a number of humans congregated below, and touched the magnification stud.

Instantly, he could see just what was taking place below.

It was something out of H.G. Wells's *Island of Dr. Moreau*. Three beings, human and otherwise, were strapped to tables in various states of vivisection. Wires and other instruments abounded. Bits and pieces of limbs and organs floated in the adjacent nutrient tanks.

Northern took a deep breath, holding back his revulsion. He had to get this over with and get out before he was caught; no time for reactions.

He clicked off a few shots then tracked around the room, looking for other incriminating shots. This was going to be better than he had imagined. Back on the *Starbow* he'd make up bunches of 8 x 11 glossies for distribution. When the free colonies got a load of these babies—

Northern heard a scrabbling sound nearby and looked up.

"Cripes!" he muttered, despite himself.

Coming toward him was one of the Conglomerates, and what an ugly thing it was: a collection of pincers, antennae, and mottled, stitched-together skins of various shades.

It pointed a gun at him and said: "Intruder! Be still and allow apprehension!"

Damn! Northern fumbled for his needler.

The Conglomerate raised its weapon.

Northern jumped to one side, just in time to avoid a yellow beam that sizzled through the air.

He brought up his needler and nailed the creature dead in what he assumed was its brain-pan. A plume of smoke arose from the sizzling head, and the creature screeched, clutched at its face, and staggered against the railing. It tilted over and fell into one of the vats. Electric cracklings and explosions ensued.

"So much for a low profile," said Northern.

He sprinted for the door through which he had entered, opened it, and found a pair of security robots running his way.

Northern slammed the door and ran toward the next. Human security officers emerged from that one and called for him to halt.

He flung himself over the railing, hung for a moment, then swung down onto the next landing, almost managing to plummet the rest of the way to a rough landing.

Shouts from below rang out. Fingers pointed. Boots rang on metal.

Northern quickly found the nearest door and made for it. He scrambled through, ending up in another of the ill-lit corridors. He made short work of this and soon found himself in a hallway that led to the slidewalk.

If he could get to a place amongst other similarly garbed humans, he might have a chance. The slidewalk had been well-used, and besides, it would take him back to the loading dock where perhaps he could put his alien disguise back on and hide in one of the trucks until Laura returned.

It was his only hope.

Still, his mind rebelled at the notion of being so much in the open. He had to force himself to remain calm as he stepped onto the moving strip of corrogated plastic.

A klaxon started howling.

People started to look around; he mimicked their surprise, blinking and gazing about, looking for the cause of all this alarm even as he stepped over to the higher-speed lanes.

He might just make it, he thought. Only he had to be careful. He didn't want to get caught right at the dock and thus endanger both Xersi and Laura.

A group of security guards stepped out ahead.

If he could just get past them . . .

Suddenly, the slidewalks, even the one he stood on, slowed . . . then stopped. Fingers of the security men pointed his way.

How could they know? he wondered even as he cancelled the idea of a shoot-out amongst so many people and raised his arms in surrender.

"Just trying to get a good story for my magazine, gentlemen!"

The guards grabbed him, professionally relieved him of both his needler and his tiny camera, then hustled him away.

"Down with the Federation!" he yelled to the bystanders.

They gave him dirty looks.

The guards had handcuffed him and placed him in an interrogation room with a disquieting amount of nasty-looking machinery which would not have looked out of place in the Anteres Inquisition of the First Federation days.

When Friend Arnal Zarpfrin walked into the cell, the first thing he said was directed to the guards: "You haven't got enough stuff on him. Chain him to the wall. I promise you, he's a slippery one."

The guards obeyed, with no concern whatsoever for the comfort of the starship captain.

"Now then, Tars," said Zarpfrin. "Perhaps we can have a longer conversation."

Northern recovered from the shock of finding himself face

to face again with his worst enemy. "This is quite absurd, Zarpfrin. What are you doing here?"

"You make it sound like it's your domain, Northern," said the Friend. "But it's mine, and I will answer your question just as soon as—" A green light glowed on by the door. "Ah, here she is."

Friend Chivon Lasster stepped into the room.

"A strange place for a reunion," said Northern, unable to hide his surprise.

Chivon Lasster stared emotionlessly at her former lover, and Tars Northern grinned back.

"I have been waiting a very long time for this moment, Tars," she said in a colorless voice.

"Oh? Why, Chivon? Miss me?"

"You are a traitor, Northern," she spat vehemently. "A traitor to the Federation. You have caused all manner of trouble in the starways . . . trouble I have often had to deal with myself in my administrative position. I naturally am glad to see you come to justice, and I naturally am glad to be rid of the kind of trouble you cause."

"Wait a minute," said Northern. "You may have me, but you haven't got the *Starbow* . . . and you haven't got its crew. I'm sure they'll carry on harassing you and your ilk long after you dispose of me or pick my mind or whatever it is you plan to do."

"Just exactly what is the location of the *Starbow*, Northern? This time I don't intend to let it slip from my fingers," said Zarpfrin in a casual manner.

"One sign of a Federation ship and they're going to be gone, Zarpfrin. And don't think they're going to be coming to rescue me, either. We've recently relieved ourselves of such romantic notions. The stakes are much too high." Northern glanced up at the array of machinery hanging from the ceiling like an artificial jungle canopy. "So use as many mind-tapping procedures as you care to."

Zarpfrin was gazing at Northern in a peculiar way. "Just how did you get down here, anyway, Northern?"

Tars Northern smiled insouciantly. "I beamed down."

"Unlikely," said Lasster. "Such technology has been proved impossible."

"Yes. They used a shuttle to get to Kendrick's Vision, and that's how they escaped as well." He leaned over so his eyes were just centimeters from Northern's face. "Where is it, Northern? And who else is lurking in the Block compound?"

"Absolutely no one else," Northern said.

"Very well. I honestly did not expect cooperation, so I suppose I should not get upset." Zarpfrin began to pace casually. "Now then, for a little bit of an introductory chat. I would hate to burn out your brain too much, Northern. There are so many other possible uses for it!"

"Fine. I do enjoy chats!" He turned his head toward Lasster. "By the way, how are you, Chivon? You look good. Haven't changed much, I think."

"I don't think that's quite the kind of chat Friend Zarpfrin envisions," said Lasster, voice heavy with sarcasm.

"No, I must say it is not. Mostly I want to have an intelligent discussion before that is . . . uhm, impossible." His eyes lingered a moment on the machines above. "I want to know just exactly what you're about, Northern. What's making you do these traitorous things after such an exemplary career with the Federation? Just for my personal benefit, mind you. I'd like your version of what makes you tick."

Northern seemed taken aback. Then he grinned. "I keep on forgetting. You think you're the good guy, don't you, Zarpfrin?"

"I hardly ascribe to that title, Captain. I recognize myself to be an ambitious individual." A fire began to smolder in the man's eyes. "But I do work for the greater good of mankind, Tars Northern. Never forget that! And if that means stamping out traitorous rebels like yourself, then I am only too happy to dirty my boots."

"The greater good of the Federation, you mean," Northern spat. "The greater good of your particular cultural and governmental system, you mean. The greater good of the power you wield."

"Northern, you know as well as I that humanity faces a challenge," Zarpfrin said in low tones. "A challenge of far-ranging consequence." He made a broad sweeping gesture. "There are civilizations out there in the galaxies, far more advanced than ours, civilizations that have survived and conquered simply because they have served a common purpose—total allegiance to their species! We are not ready to face those mighty civilizations yet! And therefore we must somehow group together again—all of humanity—into a common force dedicated to technological and mental progress. We must unite again as humans for the good of humanity before another civilization comes and squashes us and makes us its slaves. This is the threat we face with the Jaxdron. Thus far we have been successful in dealing with them, but we must be ready to deal with more powerful civilizations than the Jaxdron. And the more divided humanity is, the easier it will be for us to be conquered.''

"The ends justify the means once more, eh?" said Northern. "But surely you realize, Zarpfrin, the possibility that your vision is simply a paranoid's view? I mean, there may always be another civilization out in the blue yonder that is stronger than the Federation, but why should that mean they want our little bit of space? I'm sorry to disagree with you, old fellow, but I am too strongly in favor of individual freedom and human choice to sacrifice it for your so-called greater good." He glanced toward Lasster. "But you're speaking very freely! I presume you've told Chivon the real reason why you want the *Starbow* so badly."

Alarm grew on Zarpfrin's face, then he quickly squashed it. "She knows that the intelligence upon that ship is a threat to humanity. She knows what a pain you have been to the Federation and its goals and is aware of your activities in aligning rebel efforts against the Federation."

"Ah! But does she know about Dr. Mish and his portal!" He turned to Lasster. "That's why old Zarpy is so freaked about the Starbow and Mish, you know. That's how he found out about other—"

Zarpfrin struck Northern across the face. "You are a troublemaker to the end, aren't you Northern? Friend Lasster, there are elements to this that aren't in your knowledge . . . that I have been unable for security's sake to relate to you. Now that we are in endgame with Captain Northern, I shall debrief you fully later."

"Oh, sure, Zarpfrin. You're going to admit practical genocide of an ancient, almost holy race, are you?"

"Holy?" Zarpfrin said. "Surely an out of date word, Captain. Now I shall give you one more chance to volunteer to help us in locating the *Starbow* or I shall be forced to dig the information from your brain!"

"Get out the pick and shovel, Zarpfrin."

A security officer entered, and whispered something in Zarpfrin's ear.

Zarpfrin smiled and nodded.

"Excellent," he told the officer. "I will go with you." He turned to Lasster. "Please prepare the prisoner for interrogation. I shall be back within the hour. You may tell Friend Lasster what you please, Captain. She is a loyal and trusted member of the Friendhood."

He spun on his heel and left.

"You know," said Captain Northern, looking at Lasster with soft eyes. "I think I missed you, Chivon."

Chapter
Twenty-eight

Laura Shemzak thought she was ready for anything.

But not for this.

When she had split off from Tars Northern in the hallway, she had immediately headed toward the Heart Computer a good distance away. When she used the slidewalks and the railcar and the elevators to get there, her principal worry had been that someone would recognize her from her last stay here. But they did not—either that, or Governor Bartlick had failed to report her activities to the security section.

That would make sense. She was a high-priority Federation agent. She had been sent there to test the security system for access to the Heart Computer. Naturally, the Governor would not be eager to broadcast the fact that she had succeeded in penetrating it.

She was ready for added security precautions, though. She was surprised to find that the set-up was exactly the same as when she had last been here! Talk about lack of efficiency!

Good thing she wasn't working for the Feddies anymore, she thought as she made her way down toward the guarded area. She'd kick some butts, that was for sure!

Still, the lack of change made the process of getting into the core that much easier, and she couldn't complain about that!

Even as she slipped down the deserted corridor, she inwardly checked the fine tuning of the cyborg controls that would allow her to pick up the radio-checks, sense the proper codes they searched for, and supply them on FM and ultra bands.

Thus she successfully made her way past the first barrage of security measures. She handled the robots at the checkpoints in a like manner. It wasn't until she reached the next to last guard that she had a little difficulty.

The guard was human. And he recognized her!

"Hello, Marilyn!" he said, flashing a smile. "What are you doing down here?"

She blinked. Her memory raced. Who was this guy?

And then she remembered. He'd been a guard at the section she'd worked at as a biotech specialist when she'd infiltrated Pax Industries.

He helped her out. "Mike Moshon, Marilyn, don't you remember?"

"Oh yes. Mike. How are you?" God that sounded inane!

"Surviving. How are the folks back in biotech? I don't see them much."

"Fine. Just fine. We don't get down here much. Not much call for it."

"Yes. Not exactly your area, is it? I mean, you can access what you need." His sharp features tilted a bit, assaying. "But you didn't come down here to see me, did you Marilyn?"

"Oh yes, I suppose you're waiting to read my authorization band."

"That is my job."

Apparatus raised from the top of the desk at the touch of Moshon's finger.

Laura had to steady her nerves. This machine was new, and she could sense her inability to deal with it. Nonetheless, her intuition told her to stick her left hand with her fake ID band around its wrist through the metal hoop. She did her best to scoop out the detection waves and supply them with what they needed, then immediately pulled her arm back.

Moshon looked up from the readout screens. "Fine. But what are you going to do down there?"

"Supposed to meet up with one of the technicians and advise him on a tricky relay. Kind of stuff we know about."

Moshon smiled. "Fine. How about dinner sometime?"

She smiled at him. "Sure. I'll check with you when I get back."

She casually strode past the station with a mock salute.

Whew. That was easy. Almost too easy. She shrugged it off and readied herself for the next hurdle.

The final station was guarded by one of the Conglomerates. Exactly why they were being created—an activity expressly against the genetic laws of most planets—was still a mystery to her. She suspected it was an attempt by the Federation to perfect the human race, now that Northern had filled her in on the bit about the quest for progress.

Still, these things were hardly human. . . .

This was a subject of a sensitive nature to Laura Shemzak, what with her own cyborg additions. Just how human was she? Just what defined the parameters of belonging to the human race?

She certainly felt human enough, so she always supposed that was the only necessary criterion she needed. But still she felt doubtful and defensive when her differences were pointed out. She often wished she was like everyone else; but then she remembered the joy of being different, and perhaps, in many ways, better.

The thought gave her a much-needed spark of self-confidence. Her gait down the hallway grew jaunty even as she remained tuned for possible identification analysis beams that might be focused upon her.

She detected none.

In a minute, she approached the final desk, and sure enough, there was a Conglomerate parked at the entrance to the core computer banks. It resembled the other one, but was different. Each of the Conglomerates, it seemed, was a different combination of human, alien, and artificial elements. This one had no antennae and was much shorter and squatter than the one she had so deftly dealt with. Surely everything would be just as easy—her unique qualities made it possible for her to insert the creature's set of identity wires and jack them into her own system, allowing her access to the core.

She stepped lightly up to the Conglomerate, whose eyes snapped to attention. All she had to do now was to figure out how to get to the creature's control plate, deliver the necessary burst of electricity to render it unconscious, and then snap on its ID wires.

"Your presence is acknowledged," said the creature in a peculiar buzzing hum. "Access to core clearance code effected from previous station. Please pass."

A long, oddly-jointed digit tapped a number of buttons, and the door to one side of the wall slid open.

Laura blinked. "Uh . . ."

"Please hurry. Door open for only fifteen seconds."

Her intuition suddenly told her to start running the other way. It told her something was terribly wrong here. But she had a mission, an important mission she had promised to complete, so she overrode the intuitive urge to bolt and stepped through into the next corridor.

The door slid closed behind her.

The walls of the corridor were in a pattern of tile-like panels. Automatically, she retraced her path to where she had tapped the computer the last time, leeching out a good portion of its information.

Quickly she found it and unscrewed the panel. It was just as it had been last time. Although no traps were apparent, she was on guard.

This was just too simple.

Hit it and run, she told herself, laying open segments of her skin to hook up with the wires she pulled out from the microchip array. She would be much too fast for any alarms to go off.

She connected.

Again, her mind seemed to flow through the immensely complex data banks, and she searched for what she needed: more evidence of Jaxdron activity here, what its exact nature was, and information about these warlike aliens.

Suddenly, her mind hit a block and she was brought up short.

She tried to shut the connection off immediately but could not—something more powerful than her mind kept her glued in place, like a fly on flypaper.

She heard a voice. "Welcome back, Laura," it said. "We do hope you can linger a little while. We have things to speak to you about."

Just before unconsciousness overcame her, Laura realized who that voice belonged to.

It was the voice of Friend Arnal Zarpfrin.

Chapter Twenty-nine

She slapped him.

After a moment of shock, he recovered and showed surprise. "That's really not at all like the unemotional, always controlled Chivon Lasster I used to know," said Tars Northern.

She took a deep breath, looked around to see if anyone was watching, then said, "There are some things that have changed indeed, Tars."

"And so, are you to be in charge of my mind-rape, my love?" he said tartly.

"No. Something a little more surprising is in store, I think." She walked up to the controls of his bonds, and coded them off.

Northern couldn't hide his shock. He stood before her, rubbing the circulation back into his hands.

"There's no time to waste," she told him. "We have to get off this planet and back to the *Starbow*."

"Wait a moment," he said. "You're a bad guy."

"I don't have time to argue. Here. Put these handcuffs back on. I have a gun. I'll tell any security folk who ask that I'm transferring you to another interrogation area." She tossed him the cuffs. "You don't have to lock them. And here's your needler back, in case we need it." She slipped the weapon in his side pocket. "Now do you believe me?"

"But how are we going to get back to my ship?"

"I have a personal starship I came in. Remember, I'm a pilot myself."

He stared at her, not moving. "This is a trick to get me to reveal where the *Starbow* is," he stated flatly.

"I can see how you would believe that, Tars. And I understand why you wish to protect your ship and crew. But believe me, I shipped from Earth expressly to find you and join you. And I can prove it. The alien ships discovered by the Federation, the ones in the AI project, the *Comet's Breath*, the *Morningstar*, the *Nebulon*, the *Moonshadow*—"

"You knew they were alien before—"

"Yes, and the intelligences inside them. They've contacted me. They chose me."

A troubled look passed over Northern's face. "But they were destroyed!"

"Somehow they've escaped to Earth's computer system, where they're hiding, relatively powerless but still sentient, supported somehow by the network. They seek Dr. Mish . . . the *Starbow*."

"I don't believe it," said Northern, shaken. "I don't trust you."

"They thought you might not. Therefore, they told me to repeat a word to you. *'Isafornph.'*"

The effect clearly registered on Northern's face—surprise. "Do you know the meaning of that word?"

"No. They said you would, though."

"It's Mish's real name. I thought no one alive knew that but he and I." He smiled grimly. "Okay, Lasster. I'll take a chance and ask questions later. But if you've betrayed me you can bet that you're the first one to go!"

"I'll accept that."

"Sounds good then. You never were one for personal risk."

"You don't think I'm taking a risk now! I'm abandoning everything I've worked for! Don't ever think it hasn't been tough, Northern."

"Come on then, and let's make sure the risk was worthwhile." He put on the handcuffs, but did not lock them. "Come on then. Let's go."

A few words of explanation to the security people was all it took: soon they were walking briskly down the corridors toward the spaceport. They were silent, Northern making sure that he maintained a properly grim expression instead of revealing the jubilance he felt.

Slipping from Zarpfrin's grasp again. The man would have heart failure!

But what about Laura?

Laura would have to take care of herself. And she was more than capable of that, Northern knew.

It was not until they reached the access area to the spaceport that they encountered any trouble.

"May I check your authority grid for taking away a prisoner," a security guard requested.

"Authority grid?" said Chivon Lasster in her best authoritative voice. "I can give you my ID net. That should be sufficient. I am a Friend."

"I'm sorry, Friend Lasster," said the short-haired young man after checking the readout. "But Friend Zarpfrin has—"

"I don't care what Friend Zarpfrin has done. It is of vital importance that I take this man out to my ship."

"I'll have to clear that with those in command, Friend Lasster. And that means I must contact your superior, Friend Zarpfrin, before this is possible. I—"

Northern was quick. He delivered a blow to the back of the man's neck, then rabbit punched him under the chin, catching him as he slumped and laying him gently on the ground.

Lasster was equally quick about handling the controls of the man's station, adjusting them so that no alarm would ring to signal the guard's change in consciousness.

"I've bought only a few minutes, Northern," she said. "We've got to be quick."

They strode out onto the spaceport landing area.

Fortunately, Lasster's private starship, the *Eagle*, was docked very close. They had almost reached it when a voice called out behind them: "Stop!"

"Oops," said Northern, abandoning his guise of prisoner and slipping the needler from his pocket. He squeezed off a shot and then they began to run.

A beam screamed over their heads.

"Hey, you idiots. You might hurt a Friend!" Northern cried. Swiveling around, he fired at the group of guards charging their way.

Lasster was already at the ramp to her starship. She

punched in her code. The door cycled open and she shouted for Northern to follow her inside.

Northern managed to get another shot off before climbing up the ramp and jumping into the airlock. Quickly, Lasster punched the door closed then hurried to the nearby control room.

She gestured at the seat beside her. "Copilots again, Northern. Take us where we should go." She accommodated him by switching the engine on, using her identity bracelet.

Screens switched on, revealing Federation soldiers scurrying to placements on the starport to the rhythms of alarms.

The engines readied for blast-off. Northern plotted their course as quickly as he could in the time allowed. Lasster was busy herself throwing this switch, hitting that button.

"Fifteen seconds before take-off," Northern reported. "I hope you're erecting the force screens."

"Better," she said, adjusting something on the vu-screen. "This should prove I'm being straight with you." She pulled a lever. A purple-crimson beam lashed out, striking the nearest Federation ship ready for take-off, blowing a hole in its hull. Quickly, as though she'd never stopped doing this sort of thing since her days as a starship pilot ended, she blasted two more nearby starships.

"That should eliminate immediate pursuit," she said, face pale as what she was doing sunk into her awareness.

"Right!" said Northern, obviously pleased. "And here we go."

They took off into the sun-bright sky.

Chapter Thirty

Meshed with the computer, she dreamed.

Languages assembled, disassembled, paraded through her mind in bare binary bits. Machines, forever and ever, machines and more machines stretched out, staircasing planets to their stars, bridging stars, spanning galaxies.

Click, clack, click.

Zero, one, zero.

And she seemed stretched out on that crucifix of metal and glass now, stretched out, dying for the universe, but detached and with no pain.

Events rippled across this matrix of universal activity in waves and eddies, and she suddenly understood everything . . . but did not understand her understanding.

Cal was suddenly speaking to her. Very close.

"Hey, Laura," he said. "I'm over here."

She went to him, held him.

"I've looked for you so long, Cal," she said. "Been through so much."

"We've been played for fools, Laura," said Cal, grinning. "We've been chumps. Real pawns."

"Yes. Yes I know."

"But the game isn't over. And if we don't win, let's promise that at least we'll get out alive."

"Yes, I promise."

"And we'll be together, and we won't have anything else separate us again, ever."

"No," said Laura. "We can ride on the *Starbow*. We'll be safe there, Cal. You'll see."

"But we've got to get out of the game first, Laura. How do we do that?"

And because she had no answer, he started fading away.

"Cal!" she screamed. "Don't go away! Please don't go away!"

A very long time seemed to pass and the stars seemed to slowly shift, like spangles on a cosmic pinwheel.

Oh Be a Fine Girl, Kiss Me Right Now Sweetie, they sang in multipart harmony.

When she awoke, she was on a cybernetic operating table.

"Mish," she murmured. "Dr. Mish?"

"She's coming around," said a voice.

"Obviously, dolt," said another voice. "Are the bonds secure?"

"Oh yes, we've made quite sure of that, Friend Zarpfrin."

Zarpfrin. The word instantly triggered her adrenaline to pump, searing off the fog. There, standing in front of her, were the rounded features, the rounded body, the hateful sight of Friend Arnal Zarpfrin.

Screaming, she tried to hurl herself at him, but she could not move.

"So predictable," said Zarpfrin. "So very predictable, Laura Shemzak."

"I want to kill you," she shrieked.

"Of course you do," he responded calmly. "But really, you should control immediate responses like that. Amazing powers of intuition notwithstanding, that sort of stuff does get you in trouble. And you might hurt yourself, besides."

Her heart was pumping so fast, she thought she would explode. "Where am I?" she demanded. "Why have you got me tied down?"

It was a medium-sized room with a desk, two chairs, and a great deal of white. It looked like a hospital room—the sort of hospital room where Laura had much of her cybernetic work done, only much more spare, much more utilitarian. There was the usual complement of various machines on the walls and on the ceiling. Dials, switches, Waldoes, dollies, scalpels . . .

"I think the reason should be fairly clear, considering your reaction to seeing me," said Zarpfrin, sitting in a nearby chair and crossing his legs. "I get the distinct feeling you'd like to do something very nasty to me, Laura Shemzak."

"How about tear out your eyeballs and shove them up your—"

"Now now, you should save your voice, Laura. I really can't possibly understand this temper you're in. I mean, *you* are the traitor to the cause of Truth and Good, not I!"

"Traitor! You fixed me so that I would shoot my own brother and you expect me to be happy to see you?"

"An expedient, Laura," returned the man casually. "Computer analysis showed the likelihood of you finding Calispar Shemzak far greater than the probability of you actually rescuing him from the aliens. And we could not risk having our enemy keep him. We do regret losing him, but—"

"Well, of course, you wouldn't know! It didn't work, Zarpfrin!" she said tersely, almost victoriously.

Zarpfrin's smile was wiped from his face. "What?"

"Oh, your device worked all right. I plugged my brother good . . . but it wasn't really Cal. It was a clone of some kind. The Jaxdron still have Cal, you see. We're still looking for him. Don't think, though, that that doesn't make me hate you any the less!"

"Tricked somehow . . ." Zarpfrin murmured. "Very clever, but how could they anticipate—"

"The Jaxdron have spies all over the Federation!" said Laura. "And apparently they've used Pax Industries as a base! They could be here right now—watching us!"

Zarpfrin did not seem overly concerned, which puzzled Laura. "How curious," he was saying. "Well, Laura. I should think that they've used him as much as they can by now. Too late for preventing any kind of knowledge transference. No reason to kill him anymore. How would you like to get him back?"

"What the hell do you think I've been trying to do all this time?"

"No, I mean really get him back. That last time you were simply an emissary of convenience."

"You're expecting me to trust you again, Zarpfrin, after what you've put me through?" Laura spat disdainfully.

"What makes you think you have a choice, Laura?"

"You mean if I don't, you're going to toss me into prison here? You seem not to take into account the fact that maybe I've got new loyalties now. And you can bet your ass I don't want to work for you Feddies anymore, despite my heavy conditioning."

"You've been asleep awhile, Laura," said Zarpfrin. "We've had time to—"

He was interrupted by a frantic buzz on a desk communicator. "Yes?" he answered.

"Friend Zarpfrin," a breathless voice said. "Friend Lasster has released the prisoner. They've escaped to the *Eagle*, blasting several of our ships!"

Zarpfrin went white. "What?" he screamed.

"Interceptors have been alerted but they were on the other side of the planet. There's no way to pursue them, or to determine where they've gone."

Zarpfrin stood and he held onto the edge of the desk. His knuckles whitened. After a pause and a long deep breath, he said, "That bastard has done me again!"

So they'd caught Northern too! Laura thought. At first she was alarmed, then she laughed. "The best laid plans of lice and men," she said.

He spun on her furiously. "You forget, we still have you!"

"I don't know what good that's going to do!" she flung back. "They're sure as hell not going to try and get me back, so you can just kiss their tails good-bye!"

Zarpfrin raised his hand to strike her, but then regained control of himself. "No. I want you conscious. And now, there's no time to waste." He turned to an orderly. "Get that doctor back in here quickly."

"Doctor? Don't feel good Zarpfrin?"

"I'm sorry, Laura. Actually it's for you—and you may not realize it, but we've already started working on the implant. One of the nice things about cyborg operations is that, although it takes years to get a good blippie like you together, once you do, alterations are a snap."

She tensed. "I'll kill myself first before you stick something in like last time!"

"Unlikely," said Zarpfrin. "You are too well-designed a being, Laura Shemzak, to kill yourself. No. This time you're going to want to do what we request."

toward this end . . . but your first priority will be the rescue of your brother.

"Now, I know your rebellious ways. Forget them right now. You have just had a small taste of what will happen should you betray us again, Laura Shemzak. In your cyborg systems, we have added a device which will neutralize the effects of the drug you have become addicted to . . . the drug Zernin, which allows you to be an efficient blip-ship pilot. This device also monitors every word you speak or write or communicate in any fashion. Certain phrases or thoughts will trigger the release of this neutralizing drug—and you know its effects. Not only that, but you could well die from too much of the stuff. And then who will rescue your beloved Calspar?"

Laura nodded. She felt as though she were crushed. Without Zernin she didn't even know who she was. She knew that now, and she knew that Zarpfrin had merely tugged on this leash he had connected to her all the time: the drug.

"Yes, I can see that you do understand. And you know now how we have kept our cyborg agents faithful, Laura. You will be provided with more Zernin, by the way. Enough to last you for a small while. But please remember who your supplier is . . . who your supplier will always be—the Federation." His eyes grew fiery, his voice emphatic. "And never, ever think that you can betray us again."

Perhaps she could take the blip-ship and hurl herself into a sun, she thought wildly. But she knew she dare not. How closely did the device monitor her words and actions, after all? It might prevent her, and besides, she wanted to live. Even more than to Zernin, she was addicted to life.

She knew she was defeated.

But only for now.

She looked away from Zarpfrin and said, "You had better take me to my blip-ship, then. They'll be wondering what happened to me."

Chapter Thirty-one

Cal Shemzak woke with the nightmares stark in his memory. He was drenched in sweat. The sheets of his bed were twisted and snarled about him.

"Oh, God," he said as he sat up and leaned his head into his hands. "Oh, my dear God."

In his hands he felt the tears that were running down his face, tears he had shed in his sleep. He shook his head fiercely, trying to shake off the images, feelings, and sensations.

He had dreamed he had seen his sister Laura . . . spoken to her. . . . He'd dreamed he had been aboard the strangest spacecraft . . . dreamed that he had walked down corridors to the heart of an intelligent starship, looked upon wonders beyond words . . .

And had then been horribly destroyed.

But how could this be?

Cal Shemzak went to the basin, tapped some water, and briskly washed his face in the cold to rid himself of the clinging horrors.

And the worst of it was, again he had seen it all through more than one set of eyes. Again, he seemed to hear the buzz of some mass mind, as though he were mired into a multiplicity of thought—controlled from outside by something else.

Was it just a nightmare, he thought, looking at his haggard face in the mirror, or something more, something that confirmed his suspicions?

His mind ranged back over the memories now fleeing with wakefulness, and he knew they had been more than nightmares.

A polite knock sounded at the door.

"Pardon me sir," came Wilkins' voice. "I let you sleep late because you seemed to have an uneasy time of it last night. But you really should rouse now, sir. Today is, after all, the day of your audience which you've so looked forward to."

"I'm up, Wilkins. How much time do I have?"

"An hour, sir."

"And you'll take me to that room 27 or whatever?"

"Indeed, sir."

"I'll be ready."

More ready than they know, thought Cal Shemzak as he went to get a much-needed shower.

At the end of the corridor was a door where before there had only been blank wall.

"If you'll follow me, sir," said Wilkins, his usual manservant's attire brightened by a single pink carnation. Cal had selected his usual gray jumpsuit—his wardrobe held not much variety.

Wilkins turned a doorknob and entered a section of this complex previously inaccessible though quite similar to the rest. They walked past a number of doors, each as featureless as the last, toward an open doorway at the end of the hallway. Halfway there, Cal thought he heard voices whispering from one of the side rooms.

Whispers . . . a kind of chant . . .

And Cal Shemzak could feel a sympathetic chord striking in his mind—an attunement to the chanters.

Before he even knew what he was doing, Cal jumped over to the side door, twisted the knob, and slammed his body against metal.

He had one brief glimpse of Wilkins's horrified expression before the door frame passed his vision and he tumbled pell-mell into a large chamber, tripping and falling onto the floor.

He saw a field of legs before him, legs attached to bodies seated in rows before desks. Forty some bodies, all apparently male, all dressed in the uniform jumpsuit that Cal wore even now, facing a wall.

"What—" Cal said.

"Sir," said Wilkins. "You mustn't be in this room!"

Cal swiftly recovered from his surprise and regained his feet. The walls and ceilings were riddled with protuberances and cylinders and other projections of alien machinery. From the ceiling hung lengths of wire—wire specked with sparkling crystalline, attached to the bald pates of the quietly sitting men.

Cal ran around the group to see their faces.

Could his suspicions have been right? Did this explain his dizzy periods, his feelings of contact with others, his nightmares?

He looked and the glazed expressions of the group registered no awareness of him.

Cal Shemzak confronted forty-plus copies of himself. He stood for a moment, stunned.

"Sir," said Wilkins, advancing towards him. "Your appointment!"

"What's going on here?" Cal said, retreating, a cold fear parting him slowly away from reason and toward panic. "What total craziness—"

"You can ask the Masters, sir," said Wilkins in a calming voice. "Now please come—they await you."

"No," said Cal, unable to control himself, succumbing to the need to run. "Stay away from me." He turned to the copies of himself. "Help. You must help me!" he cried.

They opened their eyes, but did nothing.

"Really, sir—"

Cal turned and saw another door, ajar, on the other side of the room. He ran for it.

Get out of here! Get out of here! The thought pounded in his head maddeningly.

He just needed to run . . . somewhere.

He flung open the door and was about to rush through it when he realized that a creature blocked his way.

The thing was about five feet tall, humanoid and round, with incredibly large eyes, a huge mouth, and a nose like a baby elephant's. It wore a shimmering lamé-type robe over its bulbous body, and its forelimbs looked like gigantic stalks of celery.

A speaker box hung attached to its robe. Through this small mechanism issued words: "Aha, Mr. Shemzak. We thought you might take this shortcut. A little surprise for you, no?"

Strange lights glowed in its eyes.

Cal stepped back, more surprised than frightened. The creature before him looked more like something out of a cartoon than from the nightmares of millions of frightened colonists.

"You're—you're one of the Jaxdron?" he said, voice filled with disbelief.

"Absolutely and with nary a doubt, Mr. Shemzak." Its proboscis waved languidly and casually, like a gesture of dismissal. "But all that is behind us now! We have no need for puzzles and mysteries any longer. That is why we have called for an audience with you."

"I demand you release me," Cal blustered, his usual cool gone. "I demand you return me to my people!"

"Demands can be made later, good sir," said the Jaxdron, waving a purplish stalk to someone behind Cal. "In the meantime, you are expected at the meeting and we have so been looking forward to speaking with you face to face, so to speak."

Both of Cal's arms were grabbed from behind. He looked around and saw that two of his identical copies, divested now of wires, were holding him.

"Now come along, Cal Shemzak," said the Jaxdron. "The true games, games that will be heralded in the annals of this galaxy, are just now beginning!"